
HEARTWOOD

Heartwood

J.H. CROIX

HeartEyes Press

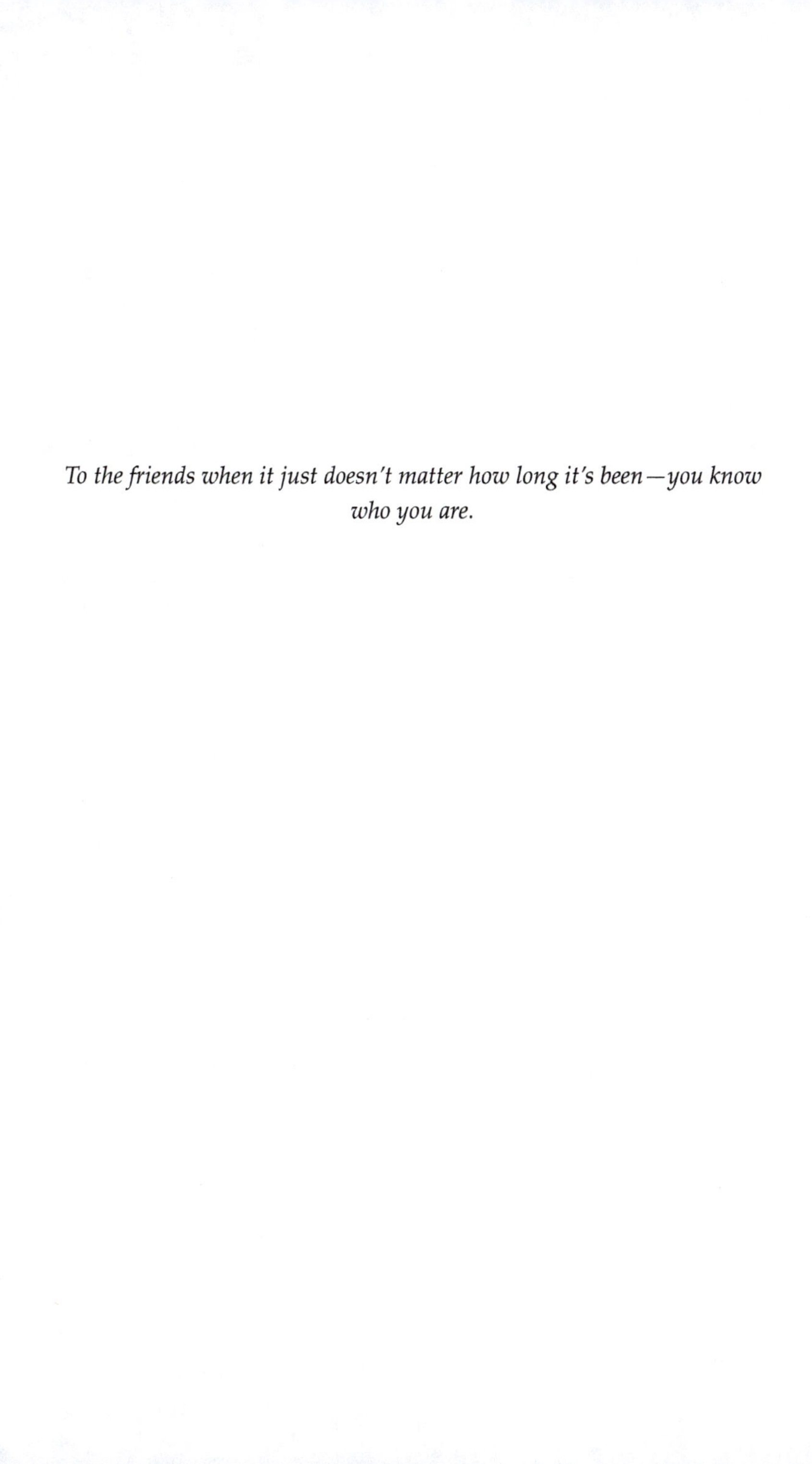

To the friends when it just doesn't matter how long it's been—you know who you are.

PROLOGUE

ISABELLA (BELLE)

Sirens flashed in the rearview mirror. For a second, I almost gunned it, but then I laughed. "No big," I whispered to myself.

Slowing, I pulled off the side of the road, gravel flying up in the air. That should've cued me to the fact that maybe I was going faster than I thought. It didn't. I felt freaking amazing. I knew I could sweet talk this cop out of that speeding ticket in a hot second.

A moment later, I tapped the button to roll down my window and smiled brightly at the police officer who looked awfully proper. He even had his hat on, which looked like a cowboy hat that missed the mark. "Hi there, what's the problem?" I asked.

"Ma'am, please step out of the vehicle."

Although I still felt great, a very distant bell rang in the back of my mind. "Excuse me?"

I was distracted for a moment when I saw another police car coming toward us in the other lane. My confusion grew when the vehicle angled across the road, stopping and parking in front of my car.

Marshaling my focus, I turned my attention back to the police officer by my window. "I'm not sure I understand what the problem is. Was I speeding?"

Out of the corner of my eye, I saw the other officer getting out of her car. She approached us, stopping beside my window as well. "Hello, ma'am, how are you doing?" she asked, her tone bright.

"Maybe you can explain," I said, looking to her, still smiling, enough that my face was starting to hurt a little. "I'm not sure why he pulled me over and now he's asked me to get out of the car."

It all seemed too much to me for a speeding ticket. Surely, they'd see my point any minute now.

"Ma'am," the officer with the hat intoned. "You're under arrest for stealing a car."

The female officer helpfully added, "That would be this vehicle."

"You mean, car theft? Like that video game?" I chirped before laughing hysterically.

Much to my chagrin, they weren't too amused and they arrested me. I couldn't say how much later it was because I'd lost all track of time, but sometime later I was sitting across from a social worker named Janet.

No one had put me in a jail cell yet, and I'd asked them not to call my parents. For God's sake, we did not need to worry my parents. I just needed to clear up this rather epic misunderstanding.

"Isabella —" Janet began.

"Didn't I already tell you to call me Belle?" I interjected. I was getting annoyed. This whole night was putting a serious damper on my good mood. I had been in an absolutely fan-fucking-tastic mood.

"You did. My apologies," Janet replied easily. She was very mellow. "Can we rewind a little bit?"

"To when?" I straightened in my chair. I could handle this. It was merely a misunderstanding. The police didn't understand, but then they brought Janet in, and she hadn't put me in handcuffs yet either.

"To your last class yesterday."

Puzzled, I blinked and shook my head a little. "My last class was today. I swear, you can check on it. Just call Professor —" I paused abruptly when I had trouble finding his name in my brain. It felt like my thoughts were rushing by, blowing like loose leaves in a fierce wind. I couldn't slow them down and focus long enough to catch one.

Janet cocked her head to the side, her calm gaze assessing me. I suddenly felt exhausted. "I'm really tired. Can I go home, please?"

"You don't seem to understand what happened," Janet said, her tone kind.

"I don't think you understand," I muttered, annoyance pricking at me.

"Let's try again, shall we?"

Okay, I was fucking done with this whole thing. "Look, I suppose I was speeding. I didn't steal anyone's car. I borrowed it. Just call Professor Talton, he'll explain." I almost jumped up and down with glee because I managed to pluck his name out of my jumbled thoughts. My sense of glee passed as quickly as it appeared, another one of those leaves fluttering by and out of sight. I was feeling a little frantic. "I need to go home. You're treating me like, well, like I'm a criminal. I'm not. I am an honors law school student. And, you can bet your ass I will be getting the best attorney I can find to deal with whatever this is."

When Janet's warm eyes stared calmly back at me, it felt as if I were crash landing all of the sudden. I burst into tears. That was the last thing I remembered. Until I woke up in the hospital.

BELLE

A YEAR LATER

I rolled my car to a stop and cut the engine. Quiet settled around me inside my compact car. I looked ahead. The Speakeasy Taproom was emblazoned in whimsical script on a sign on the renovated old mill building. The river was visible behind the building with the water glittering under the afternoon sunshine. A warm feeling spun around my heart.

I had *really* wanted this job. My nerves were shaky, but I was getting used to that feeling. I took a deep breath and grabbed my purse before climbing out of the car. I lifted my chin and smoothed my hand over my hair as I walked quickly through the side entrance. The executive chef, who would be my boss, had told me to find her in the staff break room.

I loved food, and I loved to cook. It's just I felt a little out of my element because this place was new and had opened with a splash. It was already known as an up and coming gastropub and brewery in Vermont with word traveling fast along the winding roads of the rural state.

It's okay, you're okay. That was the best little mantra I'd been able to come up with so far. It wasn't glamorous, or even remotely creative, but it would have to do. I paused and looked around, not certain where to find the break room. My interview had taken place in the morning when the restaurant was closed, so we'd met out front.

"Oh, there you are," a voice called. Turning, I saw Phoebe walking through a wide entrance that led to the kitchen.

"Oh, hi," I said, lifting my hand in a little wave.

"Your timing is perfect," she said when she stopped beside me.

"Didn't you say two o'clock?" I asked, reflexively glancing down at my watch.

She smiled, laughing softly. "I did. I've been so busy I lost track of time. Come with me, let me show you what's back here," she said, gesturing for me to follow her.

We passed by what must've been a storage room that contained an assortment of restaurant supplies. Phoebe paused and spun her arm in an arc. "We have two offices here, cold and dry storage, the walk-in freezer, and the brewing room." Pointing past the door where I'd entered, she added, "That's the staff break room. You can leave your things in there. Hang on, I want you to meet the general manager and have him show you around." She knocked on a closed door. "Hey Ty!" she called. "Got a few minutes?"

One of my brain cells fired off of memory. I'd once known a Ty, back in college, back when I had my shit together. It felt like forever ago. It was hard to imagine feeling like I'd ever have it together again.

Nervous though I was, I knew once I settled in and got to know the people I was working with, I would be fine. After my unexpected, ahem, arrest and subsequent night at the hospital, I'd lucked into a job as a chef at a restaurant in Burlington when the regular chef went on maternity leave. A friend had hooked me up. I'd loved it and felt like I'd found my stride.

Before that, my life had been a giant ball of stress. While

dealing with a full-time course load in law school, I'd been an intern in a law program, basically doing free legal work on the side, at a high-powered law firm that pushed my stress through the stratosphere.

"Now," Phoebe said, when she looked back at me as we waited for the mysterious Ty to appear.

"Did I hear you're from Burlington? What's that like?"

I nodded. "Yup. That's where I grew up. Vermont born and bred. It's a nice little city and fun for a day trip if you need a change of pace."

"Good to know. I'd never set foot in Vermont before I came here." Her lips quirked in a grin.

"Hey, Phoebe, what do you need?" The door beside us opened along with that question.

A prickle raced up my spine. I *knew* that voice. Like intimately knew.

Turning, my eyes landed on Tyler Connor. I swallowed and tried to take a breath as my hormones sat up and took a good long look. Oblivious to my state, my new boss smiled at Ty. "Come on out. I want you to meet Isabella, and I was hoping you could show her around."

Ty's eyes met mine, one brow hitching up in recognition. My belly did a little flip followed by a shimmy. He stepped into the hallway, stopping beside us. "Hey there." He dipped his chin in acknowledgment.

His eyes bounced from mine to Phoebe's. She began, "This is—"

Ty interjected, "You can pass on the introduction. We know each other. You must be the new chef."

"You know each other?" Phoebe's eyes shifted curiously between us.

While my hormones ignored my orders to chill out and started cheering at getting up close with Ty, I nodded. "Yes," I replied, my voice sounding squeaky. "We were in college together."

"Yeah, we were friends," Ty said smoothly.

I didn't know if "friends" encompassed the *seriously* smoking hot nights we shared, but it worked. All fiery fun, and no strings attached. I knew Ty very well, intimately speaking, that is. I didn't need Phoebe knowing all that though.

Phoebe nodded. "Isabella will be our new chef, mostly working the afternoon and evening shifts. I was hoping you could make sure to introduce her to the waitstaff and bar staff. I need to deal with some issues with ordering."

Ty nodded along politely. She looked toward me. "Give me a half an hour, and we can meet to go over the menus. Will that work? Ty will give you a tour of the place in the meantime. Sound good?"

"Of course," I squeaked. Because squeaking was apparently my new way of speaking. Phoebe smiled between us and hurried off, leaving me alone with my former college hookup.

The five years since I'd seen Ty had been good to him. Ty was *seriously* easy on the eyes with a tall, rangy build. He was wearing faded black jeans, the fabric molding to his muscled thighs like a caress. He wore a navy blue T-shirt that didn't do much of anything but show off his muscled shoulders and chest. He hooked his thumb in a pocket, and his smoky gray eyes met mine. The air felt lit with a charge, memories falling like hot cinders into the loaded space.

His dark hair was a little shaggy, curling on the ends at his neck. One side of his mouth kicked up in that easy grin I recalled. "Didn't expect to see you here," he commented.

I felt my cheeks heat and tried to keep my expression nonchalant. Ty knew nothing of what had passed for me in the last few years. I didn't need to worry about that. I managed something like a shrug and a smile. "I guess I could say the same for you. How are you?" I asked, honestly curious.

Ty had been a hockey star in college until he badly injured his knee. I recalled the chatter that he might go on to the pros fading after that injury. It didn't change how hot he was, or how appealing he'd been to me then, and apparently now.

"Doing pretty good these days," he said easily. "Do you go by Isabella now?"

I shrugged. "You can still call me Belle. I only met Phoebe at my interview, so we haven't yet reached the nickname stage."

Those smoky grays held mine for a few beats, darkening slightly, just enough to give a sharp little kick in the flanks of my pulse. Because we were definitely in the nickname stage, or we had been, once upon a time.

A grin flashed on his face again. "All right, Belle. Let me take you on that tour. We'll start out front."

He led me out to the bar and restaurant area, while I tried to order my pulse to stand down. The old mill had been lovingly renovated, retaining the mill's bones while giving it a modern flare. The restaurant area had tall ceilings and massive windows that looked out over the river behind it. The rough-hewn beams were visible, as were the supporting posts, which were strung with decorative lights. The space had an open feel with shafts of sunlight falling through the tall leaded glass windows and giving the entire space a warm glow from the late afternoon sunshine. The main bar was in the center of the space with counters encircling it, while there was another small bar in the front.

Ty gestured toward a man at the bar, stocking the liquor shelf to one side. "This is Matteo. He's a bar manager," he said, gesturing between us. "This is Belle. She's a new chef. She'll be here for the afternoon and evening shift today. We're supposed to be nice."

Matteo chuckled, a grin stretching across his face. "Hey there, Belle." Tall with dark hair and eyes, he gave off a warm, easy going vibe. As I shook his hand, he added, "My daughter is going to love knowing I work with a Belle."

"Really?"

His grin deepened. "She *loves* Belle from Beauty and the Beast."

Just as Ty chuckled in response, another customer approached the bar. "Good to meet you. Welcome to Speakeasy," Matteo said with a nod as he spun away.

"This is the restaurant," Ty said, sweeping his arm in a quick arc as he glanced to me.

He lifted an opening on the counter at the bar, and I slipped through in front of him. My hand brushed against his, and the glancing touch sent a sizzle up my arm. Jesus. That old chemistry was definitely still burning hot between us.

Ty, polite as ever, introduced me to the waitstaff as they passed by the bar and explained that they had staggered shifts at the bar and restaurant. "Aside from whoever's on duty for management, the waitstaff shifts vary more. It's a restaurant and bar though, so the schedule's rarely set in stone. We all pitch in and cover if needed." He sidestepped to get out of the way of Matteo reaching for a pair of glasses. Catching my eye, he nudged his chin toward an empty barstool. "Speakeasy has a ghost."

My eyes followed his, and I stared at the empty and innocent looking barstool. My lips twitched when I looked back at him. "Seriously?"

He nodded. "Hamish used to own this building. Sometimes customers complain that stool is cold. We think he likes to sit there."

I grinned. "I love that. I'll make sure to be nice if I sense he's nearby."

Ty chuckled before turning away to reply to something Matteo asked.

After that, he took me upstairs where there was an events room. When I noticed the small stage at one end of the open space, I glanced up. "Do you still DJ sometimes?"

He flashed a grin. "When I have time, but that's not often."

I followed him back downstairs and into the staff area. He pointed to the office where he'd appeared. "This is a shared office, and you might see any of the owners in here. There are four owners, by the way."

"Four?"

Ty grinned, and my belly did a little swoop. He *really* needed to stop grinning. Better yet, I needed to get my hormones to behave. "You got it. You know Giltmaker Brewery, right?"

I nodded. "I knew they were involved here. They make Goldenpour."

"Ah, you get an A, but then you always were a straight-A student," he teased.

I rolled my eyes, keeping silent on that topic. Ty was one-hundred percent correct. I'd never gotten anything other than an A in my life. Until I dropped out of law school after making a glorious and rather spectacular mess.

"Anyway," he continued, "Lyle Giltmaker's part owner, along with Alec Rossi who owns The Gin Mill next door. Alec's uncle, Otto Rossi, is also an investor. Then, there's Griffin Shipley of Shipley Ciders. If you're familiar with the area, the Shipley family's pretty well-known. They've got a big ol' apple orchard in Tuxbury."

"I've seen their ciders in local stores," I commented.

"That's the one. Anyway, you'll see Alec and Lyle the most. Griffin comes by a lot too, but he's always in a hurry. Otto stops by now and then."

Just then, Phoebe appeared in the hallway. "There you are. Did Ty give you the tour?"

Ty's brows hitched up. "Of course I did. You asked me to."

Phoebe smiled. "So I did, but it's not like I'm your boss."

Ty shrugged easily. "She's all yours."

Glancing up at him, I felt my lips tug into a smile. Because Ty was the kind of guy who elicited smiles the way honey drew bees. He had a warm, friendly vibe. And then some, when it came to the chemistry that sparked between us. "It sounds like I'll see you around."

"It'll be hard not to," Phoebe offered. "Thanks again." She cast a quick smile at Ty before waving me into the break room.

"Thanks, Ty."

"Any time." He smiled again, and my belly did another wild swoop.

Phoebe's back was to me as I took a deep breath and hoped my cheeks weren't too flushed.

2

TYLER (TY)

I watched for a moment as Belle Dunn walked into the break room. She was someone I did *not* expect to see. Not here, not today. She'd been on the fast track to anywhere other than a sleepy small town in Vermont back when I knew her before.

I gave my head a little shake as I turned, stopping when I heard someone call my name. Glancing to the side, I saw Alec Rossi in the brewing room.

"Hey, man," I said, walking toward the brewing room and leaning my shoulder inside the doorway.

Alec grinned. "How's it going?"

"Busy."

"That's what I like to hear," he replied with a wink.

"What are you guys up to?"

Griffin Shipley was standing at a narrow table, making notes on a notepad. He glanced up, running a hand through his shaggy dark hair. "Just checking on things with the brewing."

With Griffin's love of all things brewing and Alec's enthusiasm for this place, it worked out well for both of them to be involved here. Griffin also stayed busy running his family's farm and managing a small operation for retail craft ciders, while Alec bounced between here and The Gin Mill next door.

"You meet the new chef?" Alec asked.

"Actually, I knew her before. We went to college together."

Griffin hitched a brow in question as he put his notebook away.

"Belle is good people. Surprised to see her here. When I knew her back then, she was a top honors student and had big plans for law school. This seems to be a detour for her."

"Maybe cooking is her new passion. It took Audrey a while to figure out that's what she loved," Griffin said, referencing his wife who co-owned the Busy Bean Café. Her baked goods were legendary in town. I didn't know how anyone who ate her food on the regular didn't gain at least ten pounds.

"Maybe so." I glanced up at the clock on the wall behind the table. "I need to get up front. Catch you guys later."

I walked to the bar area, pondering Belle's appearance here. My brain was also churning over her. Belle was *that* girl to me. Oh, she hadn't broken my heart or anything. We hadn't even been serious. We'd hooked up a few times in college, and those nights were my most memorable by a long shot. Life had moved on, and I hadn't figured we'd cross paths again. And yet, here she was.

Hours later, I was done for the evening at Speakeasy, and I stepped out into the starry darkness. I walked around the building, following a narrow lighted path through a cluster of trees between Speakeasy and The Gin Mill. It led to a sweet viewing platform with a bench by the river. I came here frequently after I finished working. It was a nice place to unwind after the hustle of work.

I slowed when I saw a silhouette on the bench in the darkness. The air was a little cooler here from the water flowing by. As I approached, even though I didn't know for certain it was Belle, electricity sizzled up my spine and my body tightened in anticipation. As I got closer, I could see the light glinting on her dark hair.

"Belle?"

I stopped by the end of the bench, and she tilted her face up. "Hey, Ty."

Solar activated lights surrounded the base of this small viewing platform with glittering lights strung on a trellis above. There was just enough light for me to see her. Her luminous brown eyes caught mine.

"How was your first shift?" I asked, deciding there was no reason for me not to sit down. There was plenty of room for both of us on the bench.

"Good. I mostly followed Phoebe around. It seems like a nice place to work. The food is certainly amazing."

"The food is definitely top notch. Phoebe's a hotshot chef from New York City."

As I looked over at Belle, I noticed again, as I had earlier, that she had purple streaks in her hair. The light just barely caught them. Belle had a feminine, tomboyish vibe. Her glossy dark hair fell in a tousle around her shoulders. With her wide brown eyes and mobile mouth, she had a wholesome, sultry quality. I didn't know if I thought she was sultry because of how she looked, or because of how I knew her, intimately speaking.

"I thought you were destined for law school," I commented conversationally.

Belle's eyes held mine before sliding away. Her teeth snagged her bottom lip, sending a hot sizzle through my body. When she looked back toward me, her gaze was uncertain. Her shoulders rose and fell with a deep breath.

"Look," she began before a long pause. "I was, but it turned out law school wasn't the best thing for me." She swallowed. "I'm doing this now. I love cooking, and it's a little more low key."

I stared at her, genuinely confused. Low key was pretty much the opposite of how Belle had been when I knew her before. She'd been hyper-focused on her grades. I'd graduated a few years ahead of her, but I was pretty sure she graduated valedictorian of her class. She'd also been pretty wild. I recalled thinking it was remarkable how much of a social butterfly she'd been, while also being a top honors student. Her energy had been indefatigable.

"Low key," I repeated, not quite a question, but more repetition, as if then I would understand it.

She nodded quickly. "I need something low key." She stood quickly. "It's good to see you, Ty." At that, she dashed off, hurrying along the path so quickly I was surprised dust didn't kick up behind her feet.

BELLE

"May, you didn't mention Ty Connor was the general manager there," I said into my phone.

"Should I have given you a rundown of all the staff? I don't actually know everyone who works there," May replied, her tone dry.

I sighed, rolling my eyes, even though she couldn't see me. "No, I didn't expect a rundown. It's just I know Ty. We, uh, have some history."

"Ty's a nice guy. Is your history with him a problem?"

"No. It's just he knew me before my life blew up. He also might've been a hookup in college."

My cheeks got hot at the mere recollection of those firecracker nights with Ty. My life had been pretty busy then. It's not as if I dwelled on Ty in the years since, but I'd certainly never forgotten him. We were good together, more than good if my hormones had a say in the matter.

May's sly chuckle filtered through the phone line. "Maybe he can be your hookup again. You could use a little fun."

"May!" I protested. "Fun is what gets me in trouble. Ty doesn't know what happened, and I was pretty wild when he knew me."

I could hear her sigh. "You know, there's no sense in keeping everything a big secret. Just tell him what happened. I get that you'd rather not spill your tea everywhere, but it's never that easy to run from things. I have some experience in that area."

"Yeah, but you didn't end up in a psych ward."

"Belle," May warned. "Maybe not, but we all screw up. Just think about it. It's easier to tell the truth, even if it feels harder at first. That much I can vouch for."

I stared out the window in the little apartment I'd rented in the upstairs of an old home in downtown Colebury, Vermont. I could actually see Speakeasy from here and the river just beyond it. "I'll think about it," I finally said.

"You do that. Meanwhile, I need to go, I have an appointment showing up in a few minutes. Talk later?"

After I got off the phone with May, I wondered for a second if I wanted to revisit going back to law school. Because that's how I knew May, and this topic chased its tail in my thoughts every now and then. She'd been ahead of me in law school when we'd met in passing. Somehow, when she heard about my little blowup, she'd hooked me up with pro bono representation through a friend of hers in Burlington after I stole that car. Technically, I didn't have a criminal record, but the idea of trying to get back into law school felt daunting. I wasn't sure if I could swallow my pride and do it, nor was I sure if it was what I actually wanted.

Blowup didn't accurately capture what happened. It was more like a spectacular explosion of my life. My mind spun back to Ty's question last night. He'd known me back when I was trying to be the best and brightest. I wasn't an asshole about it, but getting good grades came easily to me, and my energy had felt boundless. It went from boundless to not sleeping for days at a time and not even getting tired until it all spiraled waaaayyyy out of control.

Somewhere in the back of my brain I'd known things were skidding sideways. It's just that once I started skidding, it really was like a car speeding down the highway with the gas pedal nailed to the floor. I hadn't known how to stop it.

I snorted a bitter laugh to myself. I quickly tapped out a text to my therapist.

I think I need a refresher. Do you have any openings coming up soon?

She told me two months ago that I was doing well enough I didn't need to keep seeing her every week and could plan to reach out when I needed a little extra help. I slipped my phone in my purse as I walked out the door a few minutes later.

I moved swiftly at the stove, turning a burger as steam rose from the grill. I tended to settle into a rhythm when I was cooking, one task flowing smoothly into the next. I loved the ebb and flow of the work. Within minutes, I was passing through a plate with a delectable looking grass-fed beef burger on a pretzel roll.

The night passed quickly, and I tried not to be distracted by Ty's occasional appearance in the kitchen. When I'd arrived, he was behind the bar and cast me a quick grin while he filled a pint glass of beer for a customer. Speakeasy was busy. The Goldenpour name alone had people flocking here. Phoebe also brought her cachet as a New York City chef.

Oddly enough, I wasn't even worried about how the pace here had me rushing. Because there was no pressure for me. The wrong kind of pressure tended to set me off, or so I'd learned. I enjoyed being in a busy restaurant kitchen so much that the pace was entirely different from the kind of academic tension I'd nearly buckled under.

Later that night when my shift was over, I checked my phone to see my therapist had replied. *Of course. Tell me what your work schedule is. We can meet earlier in the day if that's better for you.* She then listed the openings she had, which weren't many. *Just remember, you're doing great.*

She said that a lot. My adjustment to this version of *great* wasn't the version I'd had in my head for so long. And yet, that version had turned out to be seriously problematic for me.

As I was walking toward the staff parking area in the back, Ty came out of one of the storage rooms, almost colliding with me. "Oh, sorry, Belle," he said as he came to a quick stop.

"No problem. Are you done for the night?" I asked, resisting the urge to dash away and avoid him.

I was caught in what felt like a cross-current with my reaction to Ty. On the one hand, that pesky chemistry still burned hot, at least on my end. I thought I recognized that dancing tease in his eyes. On the other hand, I wanted to run for my life. Because he knew the old me, the girl who was hyper focused on being an academic star and shooting to the top of some sort of imaginary career ladder. He also knew me as a girl who sure had a lot of fun. Although my fun days had slowed down in law school, I still felt shining and bright, but there'd been a constraint to it that I couldn't escape.

The pressure had built and built until my plans were shredded and tossed in the air like confetti, except it wasn't fun, and I ended up in the psych ward. Stealing a car hadn't even blipped on my radar when it happened. I wasn't trying to make excuses, but I hadn't been thinking clearly. At all. It was only after the fact that sheer mortification at my actions swamped me. The funny thing was when you were manic, basically everything seemed like a good idea, no matter how horribly bad it actually was.

May's advice repeated in my thoughts. *It's easier to tell the truth, even if it feels harder at first.*

Ty was nodding, and I had to nudge my brain back onto the track of our conversation. "Yep, all done for the night," he was saying. "Fortunately, I don't often have to work the late shift at the bar. I'm guessing you're done too." He fell into step beside me.

That entire half of my body felt prickly and hot from his presence there. I should've been distracted by the low hum of conversation from the bar behind us, but the sounds didn't even register. All of my awareness centered on Ty.

"How are you settling in?" He stopped and held the door for me.

I slipped past him quickly, replying, "Good, I think."

I felt uncertain a lot lately, a feeling I wasn't familiar with. I used to feel confident most of the time. I felt like I had my shit together, and I knew what to do with my life. These days, I questioned everything. For example, was I supposed to just say good night and walk on by? Or, stop and chat with Ty? This felt like a huge question with ramifications I couldn't fully grasp.

More than chatting, I wanted to kiss him. Which wasn't a smart plan. I stared up at him, appreciating his smoky eyes, and his mouth with that dimple right on his chin. He was oblivious to the questions bouncing around in my thoughts, which was for the best.

"Want to head next door to The Gin Mill for a drink?"

"Is that consorting with the enemy?" I quipped.

"Definitely not. Alec is part owner here and full owner there. It's totally cool. Not to mention, that's a bar, and we've got the brewery and a full-blown gastropub at Speakeasy. Honestly, I prefer to hang over there after hours, just because I work here. Being a manager, I don't want staff worrying about what I do off the clock."

My lips were forming the word "yes" before I could think better of it.

"Come on, we'll walk over," he said.

I followed Ty along the path through the trees to The Gin Mill, and a few minutes later, I found myself sitting across from him at a table. I looked around the space. I'd seen it from the outside, but this was the first time I'd been inside. The Gin Mill had a funky, warm vibe with the bar hopping, lights glittering outside on the patio and music creating an inviting space.

"This place is nice. I love that they're renovating the old mill buildings here," I commented when my eyes made their way back to Ty.

"It is. They're gorgeous old buildings. From what I understand, it used to be pretty rundown, but Alec jumpstarted things when he bought this place and renovated it."

"So, tell me, how did you end up in Colebury?" I asked after a waitress stopped by to take our drink order.

I ordered a glass of wine, telling myself one drink was fine. One drink *was* fine, but the old me used to push it, and that wasn't a good idea.

"I was looking around for a job. I bartended on the side all through college and managed a place for a bit after I graduated. When I heard about this place, I applied and got the job. It's that simple. What about you?"

I fiddled with the bracelet on my wrist. It was such a basic question and entirely expected. We *did* know each other once upon a time, but that felt like another world completely. I couldn't have imagined I'd end up looking for a job as a chef, and Ty had been a hot hockey star. The only thing that carried over from that time were the embers of our chemistry, which were still burning hot to the touch.

"You're not from here, are you?" he prompted, as if somehow reading into my thoughts.

"I grew up right outside Burlington. My friend, May, told me about the opening for a chef at Speakeasy and introduced me to Phoebe. I knew May from law school. She was a few years ahead of me." I left out the second part of our connection, which was that she'd helped me find legal help at a time I really needed it. "I was looking for a job, and it seemed like a good fit. I found an apartment just down the street. I don't even have to worry about driving to work, which is convenient."

"Oh, so you *did* go to law school?"

Fuck a duck. Once again, I recalled May's friendly reminder that telling the truth was the easiest option I had. It's just I thought I'd be coming to a town where I wouldn't know many people. I sure as hell didn't think I'd run into my favorite college hookup. Not that I had many, but Ty definitely shined bright.

I took a breath and steeled myself. "I did. Here's the thing, uh, things got a little rough for me in law school. I wasn't doing well, and I kind of spiraled." I circled my hand in the air, a poor example of what spiraling looked like in my life. "Long story short, I have Bipolar Disorder and had a manic episode. Ever heard of that?"

Okay, then. I hadn't meant to just spill it all right then, but I supposed my subconscious had really taken May's advice to heart.

Ty regarded me quietly, and my stomach churned nervously. After too many beats of my heart, he nodded slowly. "I think so. What does that have to do with you and law school?"

I swallowed. "Well, the pressure for me wasn't healthy, and after everything, it wasn't what I wanted. It was best for me to drop out. I need a career that doesn't involve me feeling so pressured."

Okay, everything I said was completely true, it's just I'd framed it in the gentlest terms possible.

The gods smiled upon me at that moment, and our waitress appeared at our table, setting down two glasses of ice water, my wine, and a bottle of beer for Ty. "Do you two need anything else?"

"I'm all set, thank you," I replied.

"I'm good, thanks." Ty nodded, and she hurried off, immediately stopping at another table to take orders.

I took a swallow of my wine. I was hoping Ty would drop the topic of me and my life, but no such luck.

"It's hard to imagine you not thriving under pressure," he commented. "You were the academic queen and the life of the party in college."

He was right, it's just I didn't realize the way I felt in college was before my mania exploded. The psychiatrist at the hospital and later my therapist both said I was probably experiencing hypomania during college. When you're keeping your shit together and people don't think you're out of control yet was how I thought of it.

I shrugged lightly. "Maybe so, but everything didn't go so well. Do you really know what Bipolar Disorder is like?" I pressed, surprising myself with that question.

Ty looked a little sheepish and took a pull from his beer. "I don't suppose I do. It's like when people's moods go up and down, right?"

I bit back the urge to burst out laughing hysterically. Because, sure, moods went up and down. But most people didn't quite grasp that the highs were like no other high possible. I figured there was no need to freak him out though.

I took another swallow of wine, wishing it would settle my nerves a little bit. Between my body's ever-present reaction to him, and this uncomfortable conversation, I was feeling more than a little unsettled.

"In the most general sense, yes. I don't like letting it define everything about me, but I was able to juggle everything I did because I actually did have a little more energy than most people. That was when I was on the upswing. When I was manic, I hardly slept for days, and it didn't even bother me. I was on top of the world." I paused, my lips curling in a rueful smile. "Until I wasn't, and I did some stupid things. I spent a night in the hospital until they figured out what was going on. If you were thinking I was organized and smart and still the life of the party, you would be wrong," I said, trying to keep my anxiety from lacing my words.

His eyes searched mine, and I thought perhaps this might be the point where he got up and ran away. May *did* encourage me to be honest, but I was seriously doubting the wisdom of that about now. He didn't run though.

He nodded slowly instead. "Okay, so things got a little out of control then. Well, I'm all about doing things that aren't too stressful. That's part of the reason I ended up here too."

TY

"What do you mean?" Belle said, catching a lock of hair with her hand and spinning it around her fingers.

"I don't know if you recall, but I might've had a shot at going pro in hockey."

Her pretty brown eyes held mine as she nodded slowly. "Of course, I remember. You were the star goalie for a while in college. Then, you got injured." She paused, her cheeks flushing pink. "We hooked up before and after your injury." This time, she smiled and laughed a little nervously, but I saw a flash of the girl I'd known before—bold and bright.

"Oh, I recall," I replied, not shying away from holding her eyes. Because I wouldn't mind a repeat of that.

Dude, this girl just told you she spent a night in a psych hospital.

The minute that skeptical, bitter voice spoke up, I kicked it to the curb. I had my own share of shit to carry. Maybe I didn't quite understand what all Belle had gone through, but I knew she was basically a good person. I sure as hell hadn't forgotten our nights together. That was nearly impossible. My times with her were burned into my memory.

Belle's cheeks flushed a deeper shade of pink at my comment, and she rolled her eyes. "I'm not as fun as I used to be."

The girl I knew before was anything but uncertain, and the hint of vulnerability I saw flickering in her dark eyes sent a wash of protectiveness rolling through me. I didn't like seeing her worrying like this.

Fuck, I was getting all caught up in my head, something I didn't let myself do very often. Having Belle spin back into the orbit of my life brought an onslaught of memories, not all of them related to just how much fun we had between the sheets.

"Neither am I. Is anybody as fun as they were in college?" I mused. "Anyway, when the pro option was off the table, my dad wanted me to go into his business."

Just when I thought I was going to need to explain what that meant, Belle interjected, "Oh yeah, your dad runs that bigwig investment company. Right?"

I chuckled. "Of course, you remember."

She rolled her eyes. "I do have a good memory. So, it doesn't seem like you wanted to work for your dad."

Since she'd been honest with me, I decided to do the same for her. "Nope. My dad's kind of an asshole. Even before I lost my shot at going pro in hockey, I knew I was never going to work for him. Can't stand the guy," I said flatly.

Asshole didn't seem to do my dad justice, but it was short hand for whenever I needed to describe him. My dad was cold, distant, and frankly, I preferred to limit my interactions with him. For reasons that remained somewhat of a mystery to me, my mother was still married to him. I loved her, but I could do without my father.

Belle's brow furrowed, and she reached across the table, resting her hand on mine and giving it a quick squeeze. I knew she meant it to be comforting, and she'd always been that kind of girl, easy with affection with her friends. And yet, that subtle touch sent licks of fire chasing over the surface of my skin. Her touch was gone before I could absorb it. "I'm sorry. Nobody deserves a dad who's a fucking asshole," she said stoutly.

"Agreed. He pushed hard, but I made sure to find work

nowhere near New York City. I stayed in Vermont after college, and I heard about Speakeasy. It was an easy fit. It's a great place. Pretty tight as far as the atmosphere and the people who work there. I like it, and I like the town."

Belle nodded slowly and took another swallow of her wine. A deep red drop escaped at the corner of her mouth, and the tip of her tongue darted out to swipe it up, sending a jolt of awareness through me.

Fuck me. While I hadn't forgotten Belle, I'd honestly never expected to see her again. Now, she was up close and personal, and I was seeing her all the time.

"I have to admit I was a little nervous when I saw you," she said, resting her elbows on the table and idly tracing a circle around the base of her wine glass.

When she looked over at me, my eyes landed on the light smattering of freckles on her nose and cheeks. I didn't need to remember that she had freckles in a few other places. I forced my attention to the conversation at hand.

"You were nervous? I promise I don't bite," I teased, promptly remembering that I had, in fact, nibbled on her with my teeth on more than one location on her delectable body.

Belle had this girl next-door vibe—a little feminine, a little tomboy with her long skirts and boots, and a little wholesome wrapped up in a package of sultry and seductive as sin.

Her cheeks went pink again, and she let out a little sigh. "I know you don't bite. I was nervous because you knew me before my life kind of fell apart for a little bit there. I hope we can be friends."

"We were friends before, and we're friends now. We all have tailspins here and there, right?"

She bit her lip, drawing my attention to her pretty mouth, which I still wanted to kiss.

"Of course. I was nervous though because I thought you might think I was how I was before."

"You're still Belle, just a little more mellow. It's probably good not to be so driven. Hell, as far as I could tell you didn't have much time back then. You were always taking advanced classes and seemed to have the pedal to the metal on life."

Her brows hitched up, and then she burst out laughing. "Was that funny?" I prompted, not sure what I said that was so funny.

"Yes, but that's a story for another day. It's really good to see you again. I'm glad you're doing well even though things didn't work out with hockey. I can imagine that was a tough blow to take."

"It was. After my knee blew out, I never got back up to full speed. Life is what it is. Just gotta shift gears and follow where the road leads you."

I still missed the chance to play pro, but I had adjusted with some grace to my change of fortune in hockey. Even if the stars aligned, and sometimes that's how it seemed when it came to pro sports, there were never any guarantees.

"That's one way to put it," she said softly.

"Hey!" a voice said.

Glancing to the side, I saw May Shipley approaching our table. "Hey there, May," I said just as she stopped right beside us.

May smiled between us, her eyes bright. I'd gotten to know May pretty well. Seeing as Alec Rossi was her boyfriend and one of my bosses, she popped in and out of Speakeasy with some frequency. They lived in a loft apartment a few floors above The Gin Mill, so I guessed she might be stopping in to steal Alec away.

"I hope you're being nice to Belle," she said, tapping me lightly on the shoulder.

Belle grinned. "What would you do if he wasn't?"

May shrugged, her long dark hair falling over one shoulder as she cocked her head before shrugging just as Alec arrived beside her. He dropped a kiss on her cheek and slid his arm around her waist.

"Ready to go?" he asked.

"Yep. Good to see you both." Just as they started to turn away, she glanced back, looking toward Belle. "We should get coffee soon. Busy Bean, tomorrow morning?"

Belle nodded. "What time?"

"Nine?" At Belle's nod, May waved and spun away.

"Do you know May well?" I asked as they disappeared through the door.

"I was just starting in law school when she graduated. I knew her in passing and, uh, when I needed some legal advice, she helped me out. I got to know her better then, and when she knew I was looking for a job, she told me about Speakeasy. I worked as a chef for a while at a restaurant in Burlington, but I really wanted a change of scenery."

"May's good people. Alec is too," I offered.

Our waitress stopped by the table to check on us, and not much later, we walked outside into the cool summer evening. When I first moved up here in college, one of my favorite things was how clear the night sky was. Growing up in New York City meant heavy light pollution. Out here in small town Vermont, the stars were big and startlingly bright on clear nights. I leaned my head back, scanning the glitter scattered across the velvety night sky.

"My apartment's that way," Belle said, her voice bringing my attention to her. "It was good to catch up. I'm sure I'll see you at work."

As we stood there, with the muted sound of the bar behind us, I wanted to kiss her, something fierce. She didn't give me a chance. "Good night." In a flash, she was walking quickly away, her hand curled around the leather strap of her purse looped over her shoulder. I listened to the sound of her footsteps scuffing on the gravel parking lot.

Maybe it wasn't smart to get tangled up with Belle since we worked together. My body didn't give one damn about smart. Holy hell, I wanted to get tangled up with Belle again.

5

BELLE

"Some legal advice," I muttered to myself as I scrubbed at the kitchen sink in my apartment.

It was a beautiful slate sink with gorgeous fixtures that had lost their shine over the years. After a restless night of sleep, I'd decided I was going to make it gleam before I went to meet May for coffee.

I'd practically bolted away from Ty last night. Because I *really* wanted to kiss him. If I'd stayed near him for even one second more, I totally would've gone for it. If my memory was accurate, I was the one who made the move on him the first time. That was the old me—bold and brash.

It felt like I hesitated with everything these days. Ty knew the way I used to be, always pushing the envelope. He'd probably think I was boring now if he knew the state of my life. I'd been celibate for over a year. I hadn't actually had sex since my manic episode. I didn't even know what it would be like anymore.

I happened to glance at my watch right then, noticing I only had a few minutes to make it on time to meet May. I put away my cleaning supplies and dashed out.

The scent of fresh baked goods assailed me when I stepped into the Busy Bean Café. Pausing, I glanced around, taking stock of the space. The café had a whimsical quality and felt warm and inviting. "Belle," a voice called.

Glancing over, I saw May seated at a small table. I waved. "Hey, be right over after I get some coffee."

I waited in line while a couple in front of me finished paying. Once I was at the counter, I quickly ordered a triple shot Americano. "What do you recommend?" I asked as I eyed the display case of baked goods on the counter. A striking woman with dark hair and dark eyes glanced over from where she was carefully placing some items inside the case. "Everything's good. If you're partial to scones, the fresh currant scones are delicious." She cast me a quick smile.

"Thanks for the recommendation. I'll take one of those." The girl at the register rang me up and quickly prepped my coffee.

A few moments later, I slipped into the chair across from May. I took a swallow of my coffee. "Oh, my. It's delicious."

May grinned. "It's my favorite coffee shop. Alec's sister, Zara, is one of the owners," she offered.

"Oh, really? That's handy. Do you get a discount?"

May chuckled. "Definitely not. Zara has four brothers. With Alec also owning two businesses, they have an agreement that there's too many of them for them to offer discounts to each other."

"Makes sense." I broke off a piece of the scone which was still warm on the small plate. The fresh tang of currants danced across my tongue. I moaned. "These are divine," I added when I finished chewing.

"I already had one." May gestured to her empty plate. "Everything here is good. Audrey, Zara's co-owner, is a chef like you. She even went to some program in France, after finishing culinary school. She's married to my brother Griff. Like I mentioned when I told you about the job, he's one of the owners at Speakeasy."

I nodded, replying, "I'm just a sort-of chef. I don't have any formal training," I offered, experiencing a stab of uncertainty. This new job was fun, and I loved cooking, like *really* loved it. But I definitely didn't have any formal training, just years at the elbow of my mother who'd been a classically trained chef once upon a time before she went into law. In a way, my mother and I had reverse career paths.

"How is it at Speakeasy?" May asked.

"I like it. Everybody's really nice. Phoebe, I suppose my official boss, is great. She's nice and knows absolutely nothing about my life before."

May pursed her lips, her eyes softening as she looked at me. "Everyone has a past. Myself included," she reminded me.

I would be forever grateful for May's help in finding me a good attorney after my mishap. It helped that they had scooted me over to the psych hospital within hours of my arrest. The professor whose car I'd stolen had been gracious enough to agree to have the charges dropped completely.

May knew the entire sordid story. It was hard to go from top honors in law school for my first two years to completely losing control of the narrative of my life in my third year.

Unlike me, May wasn't stuck in the ditch of my regrets and moved the conversation along. "Tell me about you and Ty. He's been in town since Speakeasy opened last summer, and I can't find anyone who doesn't like him yet."

I cast her a skeptical look because I knew she was fishing. "He *is* a nice guy. It's just, well, I was looking for a clean slate here. It's kind of hard to get that when one of my old hookups works with me."

May canted her head to the side. "Is that so bad? There's nothing wrong with a little fun on the side. From what I can see, you're working as hard as possible at living an entirely boring life." May seemed to have volunteered herself as my mentor of sorts and definitely thought I needed to have more fun.

"May! How much do you know about my life? You knew me at law school, but not that well."

"Girl, your story traveled. Not to Colebury, don't worry about that. But you've been living here for what, a few weeks now? The only time anyone's seen you out and about in town was when you had drinks last night with Ty."

"How the hell would anyone know?" I took a gulp of coffee, needing the fortifying rich flavor and the zing of caffeine.

She grinned. "Sidenote: small towns are impossible. Plus, I saw you there."

"I know that, but how do you know I haven't done anything else?" I countered, feeling contrary.

"Because aside from Speakeasy and The Gin Mill, there's really nowhere else to go in the evening. Unless you're sneaking around."

I shrugged. "You're right, boring is my motto. It has been for the last year or more."

"I'm not saying you should go wild. Look, I'm a recovering alcoholic and will be for the rest of my life. I totally get trying to keep things mellow. But you can have friends, and you're allowed to have fun. Ty seems like a good guy. As far as I know, he doesn't have a girlfriend."

"How do you know?" I hoped it wasn't obvious I was eager as a puppy for info on Ty.

"Small town," she chirped. "Trust me, I get it, having everyone all up in your business can be annoying, but it does sort of make you just deal with yourself."

I took another swallow of my coffee. "I did tell Ty about, well, things."

""Things" is a pretty broad statement," May returned with air quotes. "What do you mean?"

"That I skidded off the rails and ended up in a psych hospital for a night. I thought he should know that right off the bat."

May nodded slowly. "Well?"

"Well, what?"

May threw a hand up in the air as I took another bite of my scone. "How did he react?"

I finished chewing and shrugged. "Okay, I think. I mean he didn't run for the hills."

"Like I said, everybody's got a story. If we were all judged on our worst days and our worst choices for the rest of our lives, it would suck," May offered. "I almost got a DUI, and it's just pure luck I didn't."

"Really?" Although May was open about being in recovery, I hadn't heard that detail.

"See, everybody's got a story. Stop being so hard on yourself. I think part of your problem is you were a hard-core overachiever. Maybe you should call yourself a recovering academic over-achiever."

I burst out laughing. She couldn't know how on the nose she was. "Very true."

Just then, a woman with blond hair pulled back in a ponytail with a sunny quality to her paused beside our table. "Hey," she said in a cheerful voice.

May smiled easily. "Hey, how's it going?"

"Good. I slept through the night, that's always awesome."

May grinned and gestured across the table to me. "Audrey, this is my friend Isabella. She goes by Belle. She's a new chef at Speakeasy." Glancing to me, May added, "This is Audrey. She's the one who probably made that scone you said was so good."

Two pairs of eyes dropped to my now-empty plate which only had a few crumbs left on it. I smiled up at Audrey. "Your scones are delicious."

Audrey smiled again. "Thanks. I'd like to take credit, but Roderick made those. Although, it *is* my recipe. It's great to meet you. Welcome to town. I hope you enjoy working at Speakeasy. Phoebe has created a phenomenal menu."

I nodded, feeling a twinge of that uncertainty that was starting to become familiar. "She has. I just hope I can keep up."

Audrey nodded encouragingly. "I'm sure you can. It'll be great. I hope we see you around here more for coffee, or scones, or plain old gossip."

"I've already advised her that gossip's hard to escape," May added with a solemn nod.

She and Audrey seemed to find that hysterical and burst out laughing together. As May and I walked out together a few minutes later, she paused at the side of the parking area. "It'll be okay." She must've seen the questions swirling in my eyes. "Life, I mean. Just think of this as a reboot. The new and improved version of you."

"I'll try. Thanks for the coffee invite."

"Of course. I'll see you soon." As I turned to walk away, May called, "Don't forget to have fun!"

Right. *Fun.* The problem with fun was it used to be my specialty. May was accurate that I also used to be an academic overachiever. But somehow, before everything spiraled way out of control, that little bit of mania was like extra fuel in my life. I had enough energy to make straight A's, work, and also have plenty of fun. I didn't even drink that much. It's just that a little alcohol with a dash of mania was all kinds of wild at a party.

It had been over a year since that fated weekend. I hadn't even noticed at that point that I'd hardly slept in days and wasn't even feeling tired.

Apparently, I said some interesting things to the police. My fun, effervescent buzz from low mania, or hypomania as my psychiatrist and therapist described it, had mushroomed into something much more escalated.

I took a deep breath as I walked down the street. I had a chunk of time before I needed to go into work for the afternoon. Maybe it was time to run a few errands. I liked that the place I was staying was so close to work I didn't need to drive, but I did need to drive to get out to that small strip mall where the grocery store and so on were.

I paused on the sidewalk in front of the entrance to the parking lot for Speakeasy because a truck was turning in. I wasn't paying attention and only looked up when I realized the vehicle had stopped. Ty rolled down the window, his easy grin promptly sending my belly into a series of flips.

"Morning," he said, a perfectly normal greeting.

My body reacted as if the presence of Ty was all kinds of amazing. Just the sound of his voice sent a prickle of awareness down my spine. His smoky gaze met mine and a little sizzle zapped through the air between us as I looked at him. Gah! Why did he have to be so freaking hot? His hair was ruffled, and he had a subtle shadow of stubble on his chin.

I managed to smile, while my hormones sat up and cheered at the sight of him. "Morning," I replied. My voice came out all breathy, which was ridiculous.

"Are you working later today?"

I nodded. "This afternoon."

"All right, then. I'll see you later."

I watched his truck roll into the parking lot and willed my pulse to slow the fuck down. I needed to get a grip on my reaction to Ty. Surely, it was because I'd been practically living like a nun lately. We had some seriously good nights back in college, but this was too much, *way* too much. I needed to work with the man, not wipe the drool off my chin while I was working.

6

TY

"You need to just tell him to fuck off," my sister said.

I laughed into the phone. "Seriously, Jess. You know I'm not gonna tell him that."

"I don't see why not," she countered. "You have nothing to lose."

"I'll take it under advisement. Now, how are you?"

"Good. It is pure heaven to have my own apartment."

I smiled, resting my shoulder against the wall inside the storage area at work. I'd arrived a little early, so I had time to take a call. "I bet. I'm really happy for you. Is everything all set? Because if you need anything, anything at all, you know I'll come help out."

Although I couldn't see her, I could imagine my sister's face, her nose wrinkling and her mouth twisting to the side as she cast me her version of a glare. "Everything is all set. It's a first-floor apartment. The bathroom is like a dream come true. You honestly don't need to do anything."

"Good. I mean it when I say I'll help, but I'm stoked you don't need it. You heard from Mom?"

"Are you fucking kidding me?"

"Uh, no."

"Dude, Mom helped me move in, she called an hour after she left, and she's called every day since. It's almost the same as still living at home."

I chuckled. "I promise I won't call you every day, and I bet she'll adjust and back off."

Jess sighed into the phone. "I know she will. I just wish she would finally freaking leave Dad. Hell, if she left him and came to live with me, I would deal with it."

My sister had been badly burned in a car accident when she was a little girl. She'd been through more surgeries than I could count to deal with infections and complications afterwards and walked with a brace on her knee for support sometimes. She was twenty-two years old now and more than excited about her freedom. My mom had pretty much dedicated her life to my sister's health in the early years during her recovery.

As for our father, he was just an asshole. He mostly ignored my sister. With me, he wanted me to go into the family business and had been trying to badger me into it ever since my hopes for a pro hockey career fell through. What he didn't get was I hadn't wanted to go into pro hockey for the money, but because I loved playing. Sure, the money would have been nice, but I was under no illusions that money led to happiness. All I had to do was look at him to know that.

"Maybe she will, but don't be surprised if she doesn't," I said into the phone.

Jess was pretty direct about our father. She thought he was a dick and had told him so more than once. He'd had a years' long affair with another woman, and it was still ongoing. I didn't understand my mother's reasons for staying in the marriage, but stay she did. With Jess finally moving out, maybe our mom would have something to focus on other than her.

Jess's next sigh came through the phone line, loud and forceful. It was more than a sigh, rather like a horse snorting and pawing the ground. "I know she probably won't leave. She stayed with him all these years. He hardly speaks to me since I tell him exactly what I think, so I think it would be to your benefit to do the same."

I chuckled. "I'll think about it, Jess. When are you going to come to Speakeasy for dinner?"

"When I have time," my sister replied tartly.

"Fine. I'll come see you soon."

"Well, I'm busy, so make sure you plan ahead."

I heard my name and glanced over my shoulder through the open doorway to see Phoebe waving at me from the entrance to the kitchen. "Gotta go, sis. Love you."

"Love you too."

"Can you grab a keg of Goldenpour?" Phoebe called as soon as I slipped my phone in my pocket. "Lily says she needs one up front."

"You got it. I'll run to the restroom and get it on my way back." Phoebe flashed a thumbs up symbol and hurried away.

Phoebe was a force to be reckoned with. I found it amusing that she was here in this tiny town in Vermont. She was a bigwig chef from New York City and had gone viral as a meme after her boyfriend dumped her at a fancy restaurant and someone live tweeted the entire conversation, complete with photos.

While she wasn't my boss, per se, we coordinated all the time. I managed the staff for the bar and elsewhere, while she was the executive chef for the gastropub and had pulled off a kickass grand opening this past summer.

I hurried into the bathroom, smiling to myself as I thought about my sister. Although life hadn't dealt her a fair hand with her accident, she made up for it in attitude. She was a fighter and sassy and spirited. I loved her to pieces, even though what happened to her mostly took over our family, at least as far as our mom was concerned. I was pretty much left to my own devices while all of her attention went to Jess. I understood it, totally, and I wouldn't want it any other way. But the offshoot was I wasn't all that tight with my mom, and Jess and I were united in annoyance with our father. He was beyond frustrated with my career choice, but the idea of going to work for him at his investment company felt like smothering myself in a cold wet blanket. I didn't want to live in the city, I hated the corporate world, and I particularly disliked him.

Bartending had been a great side gig in college. Although my knee injury rolled the dice away from a pro career in hockey, I'd fallen in love with Vermont during my time here in college. When I was passing through town and stopped at The Gin Mill for drinks with a friend and heard about Speakeasy, I had immediately put in for the general manager position. I'd been here since they opened and was finding it to be a great fit for me.

Between slinging drinks, I enjoyed the management aspect because I liked making things run smoothly, and I loved the place and the people. If there was one thing I'd sought in life ever since I left my parents' cold household, with the exception of my sister's bright and sassy light, it was down-to-earth, authentic people. This small town and Speakeasy were filled with them.

A moment later, I was hustling across the restaurant, having stopped to snag the requested keg of Goldenpour. I almost collided with Belle. She was tying an apron around her waist and glanced up as she walked out of the staff break room. Her head whipped up and the soles of her shoes squeaked on the floor when she came to a quick stop. "Sorry," she chirped.

"No worries," I replied. "After you." I gestured with my free hand for her to cross into the kitchen in front of me.

For a split second, her gaze stayed locked on mine. A charge lit the air around us. Her lashes swung down and her cheeks went a little pink before she hurried ahead of me. For a few seconds, my feet were stuck in place, but with a mental shake I kept moving and spun into a busy afternoon and evening shift.

I was in the middle of mixing drinks for a table that had just come in when I looked up to find May Shipley smiling at me. "Hey there, Ty."

"How's it going, May?" I finished off one drink, adding a garnish to the edge of the glass and moving onto the next drink.

"It's good. Is Alec around? Also, can I get some water?"

"I saw him a bit ago in the brewing room," I replied when I set the last drink on the tray, just as one of the waitresses stopped by the side of the bar to pick it up. "Thank you!" she called.

"It's my job," I returned with a quick grin before bringing my attention back to May. "Let me get you that water." I held a finger up.

I filled a glass of water for her. "Need more ice?" I asked, holding the glass up.

"No thanks," she said as I handed it over. She took a swallow before slipping her phone out of her pocket. "I'm going to text Alec because he's not in the brewing room now."

I chuckled. "That man is always on the move."

Matteo showed up to help cover the bar for the evening, immediately taking orders from some customers that had just arrived. I paused to check in with May. "Hear from Alec?"

"He ran to the store. I'm waiting here because he'll be back in a few." Her eyes crinkled at the corners with her smile as she rested her elbows on the bar and took another swallow of water.

Another customer came by and I took their order, taking a few more before I had another free moment. May took me off guard as I was prepping a drink when she commented, "So, I hear you and Belle are old friends."

If I'd thought I could play it cool, I collided with the sly gleam in her eyes when I looked up too quickly. I finished filling a pint glass and handed it over to the woman who was smiling a little too coquettishly. "Enjoy," I said, keeping my return smile absolutely not flirtatious.

When I looked back toward May, she offered, "I really like Belle."

"Belle's great," I replied, feeling like I was walking a tightrope in this conversation. It was obviously true that I knew Belle. I wouldn't go so far as to call us old friends. We'd had several *seriously* hot hook-ups that I'd never been able to forget. In fact, if I was being honest with myself, I had to admit I would've wanted more than a hook-up with Belle back then. I'd been around the block enough to know the chemistry that flared between us didn't come along often.

But I wasn't about to get into that with May. I also didn't know what else May knew about Belle. I didn't know if I was supposed to keep what I knew a secret, not just our hookup status, but everything Belle had laid bare for me the other night.

May's gaze felt a little more perceptive than I preferred. "Belle *is* great."

At that moment, Matteo called over, "Gotta sec to run in the back and get some more of the Barclay Stout for me?" His interruption was handy at the moment.

"Of course," I called. Glancing back to May, I added, "Nice chatting with you, but I need to take care of this."

"Always. Be good to Belle," May replied.

I pondered that comment as I hustled to the back and brought more beer to the bar. One of the things I loved about Speakeasy was it was always busy. I never minded hard work, and hated watching the clock when I was working. Blessedly, that was never the case here.

Despite being busy, my mind rubbed the stones of what May might have been hinting at about Belle. It was impossible to nudge Belle out of my thoughts. Not when I passed by her every time I hurried through the kitchen. As the night finally slowed for the restaurant, and the bar transitioned to straight bar service without the extra supply of drinks for the restaurant customers, I headed to the back to take care of checking on stock and making sure we had everything we needed for our next order for the distributors.

I came across Belle chewing on the end of a pencil where she stood at a counter that ran along a wall in the kitchen. My feet slowed, and I found myself stopping beside her before I even considered what I was doing. When her luminous brown eyes met mine, my heart kicked against my ribs. The air around us suddenly felt electrified. Her hair was pulled up in a bun and several locks had escaped. I wanted to brush them off her cheeks and kiss her.

A memory flashed in my thoughts—the first night I'd seen her. It was at some party in college. I was a senior, and she was a freshman. She'd glowed like a bright star. She'd been corralled into singing karaoke and had belted out a version of an Aretha Franklin song. I remembered being nearby when she stepped off the small makeshift stage. When she stumbled, I'd caught her by the shoulders to steady her.

Next thing I knew, we were kissing. It blurred from that into one *fiery* night. After that, we hooked up a few more times, each one as memorable as the first. But I was busy playing hockey and then dealing with an injury in my senior year. She was busy being an honors student, career driven and focused, but also the life of every party wherever I saw her. I gathered she didn't party a lot, but when she did, she threw herself into it with as much abandon as when she was tangled up with me between the sheets.

"How's it going?" I asked, literally dragging my thoughts out of those memories.

"Good. Just making a few notes for recipes for specials."

We stared at each other for a moment, and I was snapped out of it when someone came rushing by. The night wound down. As I was leaving, I headed to that bench by the river. I liked to take a few minutes there. The quiet was a contrast to the hum of my work nights. I didn't let myself consciously think about it until I saw her silhouette, but I'd been wondering if Belle would be there again.

BELLE

I heard the sound of footsteps approaching and ordered myself not to look over my shoulder too fast. It could've been anyone.

I hadn't walked down here hoping to encounter Ty, but I couldn't help but wonder if I might the very second I heard those footsteps. I took a breath, gulping in the chilly nighttime air. There were many things I loved about Vermont, but cool late summer evenings were one of my favorites. You could feel the impending fall coming, a subtle shift in the sense of the air at night.

The leaves hadn't been stripped from the trees yet, but the June bugs weren't smacking into my head by this time, and the crickets were a little quieter. I was busy telling myself to stay calm and peaceful. It was all for naught the moment I heard his voice and my pulse lunged.

"Hey there, Belle."

I forced myself to take another breath, but it was a shallow one. Glancing over, I saw Ty rounding the end of the bench. He looked down at me, the illumination from the lights strung above casting soft glints in his dark hair. "Mind if I sit?"

My belly spun, and I swallowed. "Of course not, It's a free country."

My voice came out husky and a little breathless. My response to Ty kept surprising me. Oh, we definitely had chemistry back when we knew each other before, but that was when I was wild and young. The tripwire of desire hadn't been flicked on in my body in a while, and I wondered if I'd gotten too rusty to even recognize it.

I hadn't made the greatest choices in men. My impulsivity had led me down a few not-so-great paths.

Ty slipped his hips on the bench beside me. My eyes reflexively looked down at the space between us, maybe a foot and a half or so of the wooden bench marked the space. Suddenly, it felt as if he were immediately beside me. His presence was *that* potent.

"This is a nice spot after a busy night," he said as he looked out across the river in the darkness.

The lights from Speakeasy and other nearby buildings reflected on the water, casting shimmers of light that rippled on the dark water. The sound of the river moving over the rocks was soothing for me.

"It is."

I didn't know what else to say and had been worrying ever since I'd gone to The Gin Mill with him a few nights ago and told him the inconvenient details of my life. It was all rather unsettling and even more so because my hormones were making a racket in my body.

Because I was me, and even though I was no longer running on the fumes of mania thanks to modern medicine, I still tended to blurt out my thoughts. "I hope I didn't make you uncomfortable telling you all that stuff the other night."

Stuff? Ugh. Eloquence wasn't my friend when I was worried. Even though I was afraid, I chanced a look at Ty to find his steady gaze waiting. After a quiet moment that stretched through several echoing beats of my heart, he shook his head slightly. "Of course not. We're all a little fucked up. I know I am." He paused, his brow creasing slightly. "That's not to say that I'm implying you're fucked up."

I laughed, the tension easing slightly in my chest. "I am fucked up, Ty. It's okay."

He chuckled. "Maybe so, but I didn't mean it in a bad way. I hope you're doing okay. It sounds like a lot has changed for you."

I shrugged. That was one way to put it. I didn't want to get all maudlin and talk about how I didn't know how to find myself anymore. I'd been so driven academically and so on auto-pilot that I hadn't slowed down enough to ask myself what I really wanted. I didn't think I wanted to go back to law school, but I wasn't sure. For so long, I'd felt like I was on top of everything and now I felt on top of nothing.

"I'm okay. Actually, I'm better than okay. I love cooking, and it calms me down. I've never been a person who liked to be idle and working in a busy restaurant certainly doesn't allow for that. It suits me."

He made a sound of agreement, and we fell into silence. It was sort of comfortable. Well, except for the thrum of my pulse vibrating through my body and the heat suffusing me from being near Ty.

I stole another glance at him and suddenly wished I could be the girl I used to be—carefree and careless. Oh, what I would give to have another hot night with him! That didn't seem prudent. But then, I kept remembering May's advice. Maybe I could use a fling. I knew it would be great with Ty. He held a special place in my memories. We had some seriously fun nights together, and I'd missed him after he graduated.

Restless with my thoughts, I stood up abruptly, smoothing my hands on my jeans. "I should go."

"I'll walk you," he said, standing beside me.

When I looked up, he was right there, all tall and strong. He was the kind of guy who tended to make me want to lean into his strength. He carried himself with an easy masculinity. My eyes landed on that dimple in his chin, and I took a breath, biting my lip.

"Belle?" he prompted.

Just that, merely the sound of his voice, sent a shiver chasing over my skin. That was enough to galvanize me. Closing the distance between us, I tipped my face up towards his. "We had fun back in college."

His eyes searched mine, a barely-there grin curling the corners of his mouth and sending sparks in a scatter through me. "We sure did."

Just when I was thinking I should kiss him, he beat me to it. I had a competitive streak, and everything tended to feel like a challenge sometimes. This was no exception. The second his lips brushed across mine, I arched up, murmuring into our kiss, "Oh no, you don't get to beat me to it."

His answering chuckle sent a subtle vibration through my body, spinning into the sensations rushing like liquid fire through my veins. The moment his tongue stroked boldly against mine, an unexpected and startling sense of familiarity slammed into me.

Maybe he'd just been a hookup, maybe we'd only been tangled up skin to skin a few times, but Ty had been impossible to forget. Just like my body remembered, he took control of our kiss. He was that kind of guy, and I freaking loved it.

Like a flame racing up a fuse, our kiss exploded into a tangle of lips, teeth and tongues, and I couldn't get enough. I was pressed against him, our tongues dueling, and I could feel the hard, hot press of his arousal in the cradle of my hips when I felt him draw away abruptly.

I made a sound of protest. "Someone's coming," he murmured as he set me back. Somehow, he managed to do that quickly but gently.

My body protested the separation, and I felt myself leaning toward him as the sound of footsteps belatedly punctured my awareness. With my pulse galloping and my breath coming in sharp pants, I gave myself a hard mental shake.

I had no business kissing Ty with such abandon. Hell, I was pretty sure I had no business kissing anyone. I needed to get my life together, not jump into a fling.

A tiny voice whispered in the corner of my mind, *Why not? A fling with Ty is guaranteed to be hot.*

I shushed that voice, and then May's teasing encouragement echoed in my thoughts. I felt a little bereft to be torn away from Ty's deliciously commanding mouth.

"Oh, hi," a woman's voice said.

Glancing over, I was relieved to discover that the two people approaching were strangers, at least to me. Ty didn't appear to know them either and simply cast them a friendly smile. "Bench is all yours," he offered, gesturing toward the couple as he reached for my hand.

Well, then. I guess we were holding hands now. It shouldn't have felt so good to have his strong grip curled around mine. His palm was warm in the cool night. I was somehow comforted, even though that didn't make a lick of sense. A moment later, we reached the parking lot, and Ty glanced down at me. "You live right nearby, right?"

My head was nodding instantly.

"I'll walk you."

See, this was where I should've said good night. Because I was, obviously, capable of walking myself home. Yet, I didn't say good night because I didn't want to let go of his hand. So, we began walking. It was only after we turned out of the entrance to the parking lot for Speakeasy that I realized anybody who worked here could've seen us walking through the area with our hands entwined.

My pulse, which had barely started to slow, lunged again and anxiety churned in my belly. It wasn't like Ty was my boss, per se. But he was a manager, and kind of, I supposed, at the level of Phoebe who *was* my boss.

Now wasn't the time to freak out, so I just kept on holding his hand as we walked the roughly five minutes or so to the house where my apartment was upstairs. The elderly woman who lived downstairs was friendly and also close to deaf. I didn't have to worry about waking her if she was asleep. I seriously doubted she would even hear if I made a racket when I came home.

When we reached the base of the stairs that led up to the upstairs entrance, my brain fired off a thought, telling me to let go of his hand and say good night. Once again, my hand, which apparently had more control than my mind in this situation, didn't loosen its grip, and we walked up the stairs together. We reached the small landing where there was a light mounted over the door.

I looked up, my eyes colliding instantly with Ty's gaze. I realized we hadn't spoken the whole walk home. I never felt the need to make small talk with him, which was nice. Although, small talk hadn't been really what we were about when we knew each other before.

Time behaved a strange way when I was around him. I had no idea how long we stared at each other, but my pulse was racing so fast, I was surprised it didn't create a wake of sparks in the air. Butterflies took flight in my belly and desire rose swiftly inside me. My brain cells were pretty useless around him, and I couldn't even muster my good angel telling me not to kiss him again.

"It's really good to see you, Belle," he murmured as he dipped his head.

"You too," I breathed, my lips moving against his when they brushed over mine.

The contact was subtle, but it felt like fire sizzled across the surface of my lips. My knees went wobbly when he dropped a kiss in one corner of my mouth and then the other. By the time he fit his mouth over mine again, I had to cling to him for support. I wound my arms around his neck, gasping as his tongue collided sensually against mine.

I had fond memories of my times with him before, but he'd taken his kisses to a new level. I distantly wondered if it was possible to almost climax from a kiss. He devoured my mouth. By the time he drew away, catching my bottom lip with his teeth lightly before letting it go, I was plastered against the door. Without him and the door, there was no way I could've remained standing. I felt the cool air filtering through the fabric of my shirt as I gulped in deep breaths.

We stared at each other under that little circle of light, and I really, *really*, wanted to invite him in. My hormones were clamoring for it. But I didn't want to be that easy. Back before I blew my life up, I'd been trying to make smarter decisions about men. I had a tendency to be impulsive, and that impulsivity had led me into a bad situation with a guy a few months before everything spiraled. In a weird way, my manic episode had neatly gotten me out of that ugly entanglement. By some miracle, I held onto my resolve to be sensible.

"Good night," I said, my voice sounding ridiculous, all raspy and breathless.

His eyes searched mine, and I wished I could climb inside his brain and understand what he was thinking. I wanted to know what he wanted from me. I didn't have much faith anyone would want more than a hookup with me.

He dipped his chin, almost in acknowledgment, I supposed. When he stepped back slowly, I felt the absence of his hard muscled body and potent presence immediately. Cool air rushed to fill the space where he'd been, and I wanted to yank him back.

"Good night, Belle."

Just when I thought that was it, he leaned forward once again and pressed a lingering kiss on my lips. A little whimper escaped when he drew away.

I watched when he descended the stairs, glancing back once more to wave. Only then did I turn and let myself in my little apartment. I leaned against the door, trying to catch my breath and instantly berating myself for letting myself kiss him. Not once, but twice.

Desire was pulsing through me, and I was restless with need. The girl I used to be definitely wouldn't have had the willpower to tell him good night. I would've had my fun and watched him go later.

I laughed to myself as I pushed away from the door. I needed to figure my life out, and it couldn't involve hot kisses with Ty, no matter how amazing they were.

8

—

TY

—

I was in a hurry when my phone vibrated on the counter. Thinking it was my sister because she was supposed to call me this morning, I tapped the button to accept the call without glancing at the screen. Big mistake.

"Ty," my father's crisp voice said.

I gritted my teeth, casting a futile glare at the phone where it sat innocuously on the counter. I was silent just long enough that my father prompted, "Ty."

It didn't matter that I was an adult and had lived away from my parents since I was seventeen years old. All I had to do was hear my father's voice and it felt as if a chill entered my body, settling like a cold ball of tension in my stomach.

"I'm here, Dad. What can I do for you?"

"I'm wondering when you're going to come to your senses," he said flatly.

He'd never been one to waste time on pleasantries, not even for the sake of smoothing over an uncomfortable moment or situation. At least not within his family. Certainly not with me, his only son, and a failure in his eyes.

"Dad, I have come to my senses. It's just that you don't agree with my choices."

My phone was on speaker, and I supposed that was for the best. I finished drying my hands and lifted my coffee cup and took a swallow.

I envisioned him gritting his teeth about now, which made us even, because my jaw was clenched tight. I opened it wide, trying to stretch the tension out of the joints.

"Ty, you know you're welcome here at the company."

"Dad, your definition of welcome is nothing I would consider welcoming. Please stop asking me about this."

I considered my sister's advice to tell my dad to fuck off. I probably should've, but there was a tiny part of me—I suppose the little boy who still wanted my father's approval—that wasn't quite ready to completely throw in the towel with him.

"How are things then?" he asked, his tone sharp.

His tone was always sharp. I stretched my jaw again before replying, "They're good. I like my job, and I'm happy here."

My father was silent for a long moment. Our phone calls were filled with these tense silences.

"How are you?" I finally asked.

"Fine, of course. Busy with work, but that's to be expected."

"You like being busy."

"There's nothing wrong with hard work, Ty."

"I didn't say there was. I've always been a hard worker." I hoped my annoyance didn't come through in my tone. I had to wrestle with my defensiveness with my father. I didn't like that he could get to me, but he sure could.

"I wouldn't know that, because you don't work for me. Most sons would be happy to walk into a high-paying position in a company that they would eventually own if only they would work there."

I wasn't going to give my father the satisfaction of arguing the point any further. "That's probably true. Perhaps, if you wanted a son to want that, you might've worked harder at your relationship with me."

"Oh, for crying out loud," my father muttered. "Just because I didn't baby you doesn't mean I didn't try to have a relationship with you."

"Whatever you think, Dad. Unless there's something else you wanted, I need to go."

The line went dead in my ear. I leaned my head back, staring at the beams above. My father didn't even really make me angry anymore, just tired.

I idly counted the beams before lowering my gaze. I lived in the upstairs of a renovated barn. I loved the space. I'd done the renovations myself. When I'd been looking for a place to live, I'd bought this old barn and an adjoining slice of property, carved out from a larger farm. I'd gotten a serious deal because the barn wasn't exactly livable when I moved in. I'd worked my ass off and renovated the entire upper floor over the summer. It was a beautiful space now.

Once upon a time in the last few decades, or thereabouts, someone had started work on the barn. There was already a bathroom and plumbing upstairs, and they'd added windows all across one side. No walls had been added, and they hadn't done anything else. I'd installed new windows and flooring, gotten a kitchen completed, and more. I planned to work on the downstairs over the winter. I loved the feel of the old space.

That was another thing my father found completely ridiculous —my interest in building and renovation on my own. It wasn't something I ever wanted to do professionally, but I loved doing it in my spare time, taking the time to get things just so.

I had refinished all the old beams and used reclaimed flooring from another old barn that had been torn down. It was gorgeous and bright with the sunlight falling through the windows. I'd built a large island in the kitchen with a subtle violet granite countertop to separate it from the main room.

Thus far, I didn't have any other separate rooms, but I'd put my bedroom, such as it was, behind a screen on the opposite end of the expansive space from the kitchen. I'd installed a large wood stove in the center of the area, which cast heat in all directions.

That was merely for extra heat because I also had a highly efficient propane stove that provided hot water on demand.

My phone vibrated again. This time, I wisely checked the screen to confirm it was my sister before tapping to accept the call.

"Hey, Jess," I said in greeting.

"Hey, how's it going?"

"Fine, you?"

"Good, good. I need a favor."

"What's that?"

"I could use a little help setting up the shelving in my apartment."

"How about I come over this weekend? I should have time on Saturday morning."

"That would be awesome. Are you sure you don't mind?"

"Of course, not. I told you to let me know if you needed any help."

"I know, I know, but…" Her words trailed off, and I could imagine her shrugging.

My little sister was stubborn and outspoken and wildly independent. She hated asking for help as a result.

"You know I hate asking for help," she added, voicing my train of thought.

"Oh, I know," I teased.

Jess's annoyed sigh filtered through the phone line. "Heard from mom or dad recently?"

"Dad called this morning, just a few minutes ago. I thought it was you so I answered without looking. Lesson learned."

Jess chuckled. "Serves you right. He's gonna keep badgering you until you tell him to fuck off."

"Probably. I will when I'm ready. How is it to finally be in your own place for a few weeks now?"

"It's fucking heaven. While you've got dad hounding you about working for him, at least you don't have mom calling you to make sure you're okay every other day. I swear to God, she needs to go to therapy. I have been fine for years."

I grinned. "It probably would help her," I said dryly.

"Well bro, I gotta go. I've got an online meeting for work. Why don't you text me what time you can come Saturday?"

"You got it."

"And if it turns out you're too busy, that's totally fine," she added, stubbornly in my opinion.

"I'm not gonna be too busy, Jess. I'll see you Saturday morning, probably around ten, but I'll text to confirm."

After I got off the phone, I finished my coffee and got ready for work. As I drove into town, Belle sashayed into my thoughts. I didn't know if she'd be working today, but I hoped she would. The mere thought of her sent electricity sizzling in my veins.

College was college, and my focus hadn't been on romance then. Even so, my encounters with her stood out in stark, vivid recollection. Because they'd been sizzling and unforgettable. Having her spin back into my orbit now only sharpened the outlines of my memories. I didn't know if pursuing her was smart. It was certainly complicated by us working together and further complicated by her revelations.

BELLE

"Mom, I'm doing great," I insisted.

"I know you are," my mother said. "I don't mean to mother hen you, but it was nice having you a little closer."

I was glad we were on the phone and my mother couldn't see me when I rolled my eyes. "Mom, I'm less than an hour away."

"I know." I could practically see the wrinkle between her brows and the polite worry on her face. "So, tell me how it's going at your new job," she said brightly.

"It's going well. I like it. It's fun to be working in a new restaurant that's off to a strong start."

"Do you like your boss? She's a big deal chef, so I hear."

"Phoebe's great. She's very supportive. She's really creative as far as the menu and has given me the go-ahead to come up with specials and so on."

"Are you thinking this is something you want to do long-term? Because, you know your father and I will support whatever you want. If you want to go to culinary school, we're on board with that."

I had to bite the insides of my cheeks to keep from replying right away. My parents, bless their hearts, were doing their very best to adjust to some big changes in my life. They were both incredibly smart and academically successful. My mother was on the faculty at Burlington University, and my father was a highly successful environmental lawyer. All my life, all I'd ever wanted to do was follow in their footsteps. I never even questioned it. School had come easily to me, and I'd been an academic star all the way through college and into law school.

Until the pressure and stress and anxiety got too much and the Bipolar Disorder that had been waiting in the wings morphed into a full-blown manic episode. My poor parents didn't know what to do when I landed in a psych hospital. I went to stay with them after that night.

As accomplished as they were, they had no idea what to do with me in my new situation. Helping their wayward daughter clean up the mess she'd made for herself hadn't been on their bingo cards. Ever.

My shame about the situation had pushed me into trying to find anyone but my parents' legal friends to help me. It was such a blessing when May heard what happened and reached out to me. We hadn't been close then, but we were connected enough that she knew I would need a lawyer and put me in touch with that pro bono program. My parents would've gladly paid for some high-end attorney, but that wasn't what I wanted.

"Mom, I don't think school is in the cards for me right now," I said, my voice soft.

My mother was quiet long enough that I knew she was trying to find the right thing to say. "I understand, we only want to support you," she finally said.

"I know, Mom." Ugh. My parents loved me, and that was such a gift. Yet, I felt like I'd let them down horribly and kept trying to find my way to the other side of that feeling. "Putting pressure on myself is not a great plan right now. Maybe I'll get to a place where I might reconsider school, but right now, I like my job. I know I've let you down."

My mother immediately cut in. "Absolutely not! Darling, you haven't let us down. We just want you to be happy."

I bit back a sigh. "I'm doing well, Mom. Let's not worry about planning for something else right now. Okay?"

"I understand. I get ahead of myself, and old habits die hard. We love you exactly the way you are, so please stop saying that you've let us down. You absolutely have not."

"Okay. I love you too, Mom. I need to go in a minute," I said, even though that wasn't exactly true.

"All right, then. Is it okay if we come for dinner at the restaurant soon?"

"Of course. Just give me a heads up when you're coming."

"I'll talk to your father and text you. Love you."

"Love you too."

I tapped to end the call and leaned my head back against the sofa with a sigh. My throat felt tight with emotion and a tear rolled down my cheek. Sometimes, it was hard to love my parents and feel like I'd let them down so spectacularly.

I'd always felt so proud, so ready to follow in their footsteps, one way or another. Instead, I'd fucked up, rather gloriously, or ingloriously. The only saving grace was somehow I'd found another path for myself.

"Fuck," I muttered.

Another thing that sucked about all of this was the very medication that helped me not spin out of control took away that little bit of the magic that gave me a boost and juiced my confidence in times when I doubted myself. Mania could feel amazing except it had a serious downside.

I pressed my palms to my eyes, swiping the tears away before lifting my phone again. I pulled up my therapist's number and quickly texted her. I hadn't been able to confirm a time with her yet since I'd last texted. Maybe I wasn't seeing her every week now, but I knew I needed support when I was feeling shitty.

The year leading up to everything skidding sideways so badly had been crowded with warning signs along the way. It was like driving through a narrow highway in the mountains that had signs about falling rocks. Pressure, juggling too much, and my asshole of an ex-boyfriend had all been falling rocks. Luckily for me, that ex wanted nothing to do with a girl who ended up in the hospital. I had so much shame about him. I wasn't quite sure how I ended up with him. He'd been another guy I thought was cute. In my bold, slightly manic fashion I'd hit on him one night, and then we had crappy sex.

For some stupid reason, I stayed with him for a few months after that, during which he hit me three times. God, just thinking about the fact that I stayed after the first hit still swamped me with another wave of shame.

I took a shaky breath after hitting send on that text and stood from the couch. For some reason, my thoughts immediately went to Ty. When I boldly approached him back in college, at least it hadn't been bad sex. To the contrary, it had been freaking amazing. I flushed all over just thinking about our kisses the other night.

I couldn't imagine he'd want more than something casual with me, especially after I blurted out the messy truth to him. I kicked those thoughts to the curb. I did *not* need to be wanting more with Ty, or anyone.

As I crossed my small living room, my phone vibrated in my hand. I glanced down to see the times my therapist offered up next week. Luckily for me, she was only a half hour away. I pulled up my work schedule and cross-checked first before confirming a time.

I decided some coffee at Busy Bean was in order. I needed something to cheer me up before I went to work.

I took a bite of my scone, savoring the burst of flavor from the currants scattered through it. The texture was absolutely perfect, a little dry, but not too crumbly, buttery goodness with a subtle sweetness laced through it.

Zara was passing by and cast me a quick smile as she gathered up some empty plates and coffee cups from a table nearby. "These are amazing," I called over.

"Aren't they though?" she returned. "I have to pace myself working here, or I'll put on a ton of weight."

I almost laughed out loud at that. Zara didn't have any extra weight on her. "I don't think you need to worry," I offered.

Just then, a tall man with coppery red hair came striding into the café. He was hard to miss, handsome and obviously built. The man scanned the café quickly, his eyes landing on Zara. He crossed over, stopping beside the table. "Hey, gorgeous."

Zara's cheeks went a little pink. "Hey, where are the kids?"

"Dropped them off with your mom. I was going to head over for lunch yoga class and thought I'd see if you wanted to go."

Zara opened her mouth to reply when Audrey hurried by. "Just go. You need a break."

The man who I was guessing was Zara's husband waggled his eyebrows. Zara rolled her eyes. "Okay, I'll go."

Zara glanced to me. "This is Dave, my husband." She gestured between us. "This is Belle. She's a new chef at Speakeasy."

Dave flashed a grin at me. "Nice to meet you."

I couldn't say why, but he looked familiar. When I looked a little too curiously, Zara added, "If you're a hockey fan, you might recognize him. He used to play hockey for the Brooklyn Bruisers."

"Oh, that's why you look familiar. I'm not a diehard fan, but I do follow hockey. I am from Vermont, after all," I offered with a shrug.

Dave nodded. "Vermont's a hockey kind of state even though they don't have a pro team here." Glancing to Zara, he pressed, "You coming with me, or what?"

"Let me finish cleaning up these tables. I'll meet you outside in a few minutes."

"I'll grab a coffee to go," Dave said.

"Before yoga?" Zara teased.

He grinned. "I need my energy."

As he crossed over to the counter where the new barista was

getting trained by Audrey, Zara picked up my empty scone plate. "Good to see you again."

"I already figured out the best coffee in town is here." I drained the last bit of my coffee and stood to leave. When I was passing the counter, Audrey called out, "We have fresh muffins."

Glancing over my shoulder, I couldn't resist. "What kind?" I angled to the counter, stopping beside it.

"Do I get one?" Dave prompted as he handed over some money for his coffee to the barista.

Audrey nodded. "If you want to buy one, of course."

Dave pulled out another bill and handed it over just as Zara rounded to the back of the counter with her tray filled with dishes. She snorted.

After handing Dave a muffin in a small bag, Audrey glanced to me, answering my question, "Pear ginger."

Who could turn that down? Certainly not me. In another moment, I'd paid and took a bite of the warm muffin.

"Oh my God, those are incredible," I commented after I finished chewing.

Dave chuckled. "Everything they make here is good."

Audrey smiled between us. "Thank you."

At that, I glanced at my watch. "Oh, I need to go. I'll catch you all later."

When I was walking out, my eyes landed on a phrase written in chalk on one of the supporting posts. *Take a leap of faith, instead of a leap of doubt.*

BELLE

Only a day later, that phrase danced through my thoughts when I arrived at work and promptly discovered how impossible it was to ignore my reaction to Ty when he was at work with me. It seemed like every time I turned around, my eyes landed on him. He was always on the move, busy making drinks at the bar, hurrying through the restaurant to help with one thing or another, and so on. To make matters even more inconvenient for the state of my libido, he kept coming back to collect stock for the bar in the cold storage area right beside the kitchen.

At one point, he stopped beside me where I was prepping a sauce for a special. "What's that?"

I was pretty sure he wasn't trying to be flirtatious, but the low rumble of his voice sent a prickle chasing down my spine. When I looked up and my eyes collided with his, my hormones let out a little squeal, so very happy to see him.

I swallowed, willing my pulse to slow down. "Gravy to go with poutine and spicy fries."

"Looks good."

"Uh-huh," I managed. Seriously, this guy robbed me of basic speech sometimes.

I tried to keep my attention on what I was doing, but my eyes had a mind of their own and swung to him again, promptly landing on his lips. At which point, I remembered just how deliciously good they felt on mine and heat suffused me. Then, I reached to lift the pan, my hand landing too far up on the handle and almost burning myself in the process. "Ouch!"

"You okay there, Belle?" Phoebe asked as she dashed across the kitchen.

"Yep," I called, looking up at Ty again. "Busy here," I murmured.

His palm brushed lightly on my lower back as he moved away. "That you are. I'll leave you to it," he murmured.

Jesus. I shouldn't have kissed him the other night. Not once, but twice. Ty tempted me to stumble off the path of keeping my life together and not doing anything impulsive. Impulsive was such a temptation for me. With him, tumbling would be nothing more than a hot hookup, and that was everything I didn't need. Relationships weren't on this path either. I couldn't even imagine a relationship. My brief brush with one had been a disaster. I couldn't imagine anyone wanting to have a relationship with me, the girl who'd gotten arrested and who'd only gotten out of it because I'd ended up spending a night in the hospital instead of jail.

I was still trying to figure out why Ty even kissed me the other night. Surely, he thought I was a mess.

I could see my therapist giving me the side eye at this train of thought. She knew me well enough that she didn't hold back. This would be when she reminded me that everyone carried their own challenges, and that we all functioned on a continuum. She also insisted the concept of normal was a social construct and frequently reminded me to stop comparing myself to others. My continuum happened to include being very high functioning, and only stumbling off of that when I landed too far in the pressure zone.

Just thinking about this made me feel almost itchy. I didn't quite know how to let go of the way I looked at myself. Being super high functioning was what made me feel good about myself. The pressure had been exhausting and the anxiety had pushed me higher and higher into mania.

Trying to learn how to be more relaxed and forgiving of myself wasn't easy. I didn't know how to feel confident without being an academic star. It wasn't working out so well.

I still had tons of energy, and I truly did love to cook. It gave me something to focus on and, conveniently, restaurants tended to demand a fast pace. No one thought anything of it when I was racing around, and I welcomed the long hours. The blessing was I didn't get anxious cooking. I was a little anxious about impressing Phoebe because she was kind of a rock star chef, and I wanted to be good enough.

As if she read my mind, she buzzed over, stopping by my shoulder. "Tonight's special is delicious."

"It is?"

She cocked her head to the side, pursing her lips slightly. "Yes. Stop worrying so much. You're doing great." She hurried off because there wasn't much time to linger on anything when the restaurant was hopping.

I stayed busy enough for the rest of my shift that I managed not to think too much about Ty. I was leaving later that night and found my feet aiming toward the bench by the river. I told myself it was only because I liked sitting by the river for a few minutes. After the cacophony of the kitchen, listening to the leaves rustle in the trees and the water roll over the rocks was relaxing. All of that was completely true. However, there was a teeny, tiny corner of my mind that wondered if maybe I would see Ty again.

TY

The door to the back of Speakeasy swung shut behind me, and my footsteps crunched on the gravel as I walked into the parking lot. The sounds from the bar and restaurant were muted, and I stopped, leaning my head back to look up at the stars. The night was clear, and the air crisp with a hint of woodsmoke.

I took a deep breath, letting it out as I brought my gaze forward and began walking toward my truck. I had to pass by the narrow path that led to the small bench on the viewing platform by the river. I was trying to be sensible about Belle, but my body wasn't listening to sensible. My feet went in that direction all on their own.

I wasn't sure if kissing her was a mistake, just as I wasn't sure if wanting her was wise. With Belle, I wanted more than what we had before—the hottest hookup *ever* wasn't enough anymore.

Yet, I knew she was going through stuff, if stuff could describe what was going on for her. I had actually looked up Bipolar Disorder online the other day. I discovered there were some pretty famous people, who had lives and jobs and kids and families, dealing with it.

A few leaves on the ground crunched under my feet. It was early fall, and we weren't quite to the leaf peeping phase and the aftermath when the colors faded and the leaves fell to carpet the ground everywhere. When I saw the small clearing with the lights twinkling in the darkness, I wasn't surprised to see Belle's familiar silhouette.

It felt as if a bell rang in my body, the awareness of her presence echoing. She turned, the light catching on one of the purple streaks in her hair. I rounded the bench, stopping in front of her. "Mind if I sit?"

Wordlessly, Belle shook her head. Her wide brown eyes tracked me. She looked at me quietly, just long enough that I thought she was going to tell me she did mind me sitting down. But then, her lips curled in a slow smile. "Of course not. It's a public bench."

I sat and angled to face her. "Oh, so that's why I get to join you? Because it's a public bench?"

With nothing more than the glittery lights around us, it was hard to tell if she blushed, but I was pretty sure she did. "I don't suppose I want to share the bench with a stranger. It's kind of small."

The distance between us was perhaps a foot, if that. "Now that you've been here a little longer, how are you liking Speakeasy?"

"I like it." She paused, and I heard her swallow. "A lot, actually."

When she looked over at me, her expression was a little bashful and uncertain, so different from the way I'd known her before. She still had that bright spark. When I saw her hurrying around the kitchen and laughing with the line cooks—who were all enchanted by her, because she carried a light, easy charm—I saw glimmers of the girl I'd known before.

"What about you? How long have you even been working here?"

"I got hired when they were planning the opening. It was a big to-do. Hell, between the Giltmaker Brewery being involved and the Shipley and Rossi families part of it, it was big news in this small town. Plus, they hired Phoebe to handle the opening, so she brought her New York City cachet to the whole thing."

"How did it go?"

"We were slammed. I think my role was far less stressful than Phoebe's. All I had to do was make sure we had enough alcohol, enough staff and help out at the bar."

Belle nodded, and we fell into quiet. She lifted her hand, catching a lock of her hair and spinning it around her fingers. With her legs crossed, her foot bounced lightly. I recalled her being a bundle of energy, almost always in motion, like a hummingbird.

I smiled at my recollection, and she asked, "What's funny?"

"I was remembering how you were always moving fast."

She dropped her hand quickly to her lap, lacing her fingers together. Her foot went still. I swiftly realized I didn't like that she felt uncomfortable around me.

Because sometimes my mouth got ahead of my brain, I heard myself asking, "Are you nervous?"

She let out an annoyed huff, twisting her lips to the side when she looked over at me. "Not nervous, exactly. More restless, I suppose."

I caught her hand in mine as she moved to stand. "Don't go."

She shifted her hips back on the bench, biting her bottom lip as her eyes searched my face. "I don't know if it's a good idea that I kissed you the other night," she said, her voice a little frayed around the edges.

My heart gave a funny twist in my chest, followed by a sweet, sharp ache I didn't recognize. Maybe I hadn't forgotten Belle, but I hadn't had illusions about her, or us, before. I'd been focused on my hockey career that died a quick death, and then casting about for what I was going to do while fending off my father.

Meanwhile, Belle had been a freshman, bursting into college and focused on her grades with a fierce level of determination. She seemed to do everything—taking extra classes, making honors, participating in pre-law organizations, and so on. All the while, she juggled a busy social life. Neither one of us had been focused on anything but good fun with each other. But, fuck me, that fire between us burned hot. It still did.

It's just now I wanted to take care of her. A sense of protective-ness simmered under the surface when I was around her. I didn't like seeing her worried.

When she spoke, she startled me. "I feel kind of like a hot mess most of the time. You knew me when I had my shit together, so I guess I get a little restless around you."

"Does anybody really have their shit together all the time, Belle?"

She rolled her eyes. "Don't get all philosophical on me, Ty Connor."

"I'm not trying to be philosophical. So, things are different for you. Newsflash, same for me. I thought I might be destined for hockey greatness. Instead, I'm managing a bar and slinging drinks, and I actually kinda like it."

She threw her head back. Belle had a throaty, deep laugh, and the sound of it sent a jolt of lust through me. When she brought her eyes to mine again, the uncertainty had been chased away from her eyes. Her gaze sobered. "In all honesty, how was that adjustment?"

"Look, when you're playing at a high-level in sports, no matter the sport, of course you want to imagine pro is a real option. Players get that good, usually, because they love it. I fucking loved playing hockey. Still do. I help coach a local league here. It's fun, and I get to skate. Even if I hadn't been injured, there were no guarantees. Plus, the glory is short-lived. I'm friends with Dave Beringer. I don't know if you met him, but he's married to Zara."

She nodded. "I met him when I was there getting coffee."

"He had a great career, and he's pretty comfortable financially. I wouldn't complain if that were the case for me, but he has a different life these days and he seems more than good with it. Sure, maybe it would've been amazing if I went pro, but I didn't. I'm pretty happy with where I've landed. Even if money makes things more comfortable, I have enough. I also know money doesn't make people happy."

Belle was watching me intently, biting her bottom lip the whole time. It was disarmingly distracting because the sight of her teeth denting that plump, pink surface made me want to kiss her. I kicked my brain back onto track. We were having a serious conversation. I didn't need to be dwelling on kissing fantasies.

If that didn't say it all though. With Belle, it was *so* freaking good, I could kiss her for hours.

"Money definitely isn't everything. I put so much pressure on myself with academics that by the time I got to law school, I just couldn't keep all the balls in the air anymore. That's not to say pressure is the reason I have Bipolar Disorder, but it didn't help me at all."

I nodded along, because maybe I didn't understand exactly what she was talking about, but I understood the broad strokes. It reminded me of the situation I was determined to avoid with my father. Because if I were to work for him, hell, we'd probably come to blows, and I didn't need that kind of misery in my life.

"So, you landed in a good spot then."

She was quiet, her lashes dropping when she looked out toward the river. The ripples on the water had a pearly shimmer from the lights glittering above us. She turned back to me, a smile unfurling slowly on her face. "You're right," she said with a firm nod.

"What?" I prompted.

"That not everybody keeps their shit together all the time."

"It's not exactly a brilliant point," I offered dryly.

"Maybe, but I needed the reminder."

She reached out, tapping her fingers lightly on my forearm. It was a playful gesture, and I didn't think she meant for it to be sexual. It's just that when it came to Belle, my body felt like an engine running on high idle, just waiting for a little pressure on the gas pedal.

Her touch also elicited a flash of memory, bright and vivid.

"You did that before." My words slipped out before I could think to stop them.

Belle dropped her hand away, and her eyes widened. "What do you mean?"

"The night I met you. You said you were playing piano on my forearm."

There she went with that laugh again, and lust sizzled through me. Again. It was like a tide cresting inside of me.

"I actually remember that, now that you mention it." Her smile was bright, and then she went and bit her lip again.

That did it. All I had to do was lean over. She was right there with her face tilted up toward me. It was so easy. I dipped my head, and my lips came against hers. Seeing as I wasn't really thinking—hell, I didn't do a whole lot of that when I was too close to Belle—I couldn't say what I meant for that kiss to be. But it got *real* hot, *real* fast.

BELLE

The second Ty's lips met mine, it felt as if a little sizzle of fire passed from him to me, that flame spinning into the liquid need already sliding through my veins. Maybe it wasn't sensible, maybe it was colossally stupid, but kissing Ty was just the *best*. It was also a rather glorious kiss.

I could forget everything but the masterful glide of his tongue against mine and the way his hand slipped around my neck to cup it lightly. He had this way of making me want to take control, but also making me want to surrender. Because, sweet hell, he was a spectacular kisser.

I remembered hot nights with him, I remembered more than one climax every time, and I remembered completely forgetting myself with him before. Forgetting myself was hard for me to do, even when I was dancing along the edge of my wildness.

Somehow, I found myself shimmying into his lap. I wanted to blame him, but I was pretty sure it was all my fault. I simply wanted to be closer to all of that delicious muscle. Ty was a big man, tall and rangy, and he had a great lap. I twined my arms around his neck, gasping when I felt the hard, hot length of his arousal under my bottom.

I couldn't resist wiggling a little. Ty broke free of our kiss, gulping in a loud breath of air as I took deep, ragged breaths. The cool, crisp autumn air was a balm to the heat racing through me.

"Fuck, Belle," he murmured, dropping his forehead to my shoulder.

I could feel the motion of his lips right over my collarbone, and a tingling sensation skated over my skin from that subtle brush of contact.

He lifted his head, his eyes catching mine. "Come home with me tonight."

A teeny, tiny, and let's face it, *really* weak voice inside of me, tried to put up a protest. I wasn't going to be impulsive anymore, I wasn't going to do rash, foolish things. But my hormones were much louder than that voice of reason. There was that, and the fact it felt so good to be with him. I could lose myself, and it would be glorious. Because mere kisses were glorious, and I hadn't forgotten how blazing hot our hookups were before, even if it had been a few years. Really great sex didn't come along very often. Most women knew that inconvenient fact.

"Okay," I whispered.

"Oh, thank God," he said, rather fervently.

"Since when did you become reverent?" I teased.

He chuckled, and I felt the rumble of it through my entire body. "There's a place for reverence, especially when it comes to you."

He gave me a fast kiss and then stood swiftly, lifting me off his lap and setting my feet on the ground, almost effortlessly. He reached for my hand as we walked along the dark pathway through the trees, and I remembered something else I'd loved about him. He was affectionate, and I'd always felt he was going to make sure I was taken care of. He wasn't a careless, user kind of guy.

When we got to the parking lot, my uncertainty slammed into me. I didn't even know where his truck was parked, or where he lived. Just as that uncertainty threatened to engulf me, Ty's thumb brushed along the outer edge of my wrist as he murmured, "This way."

That's how easily this man affected me. The subtle brush of his thumb on my wrist and the rumble of his voice sent blazing shivers through me from head to toe. I didn't want to let go of his hand, and I really, *really* wanted to lose myself in him.

A few minutes later, he was driving. Just driving. And yet, my eyes were looking at the way his hand rested on the steering wheel, and the flex of his forearm as he turned down a side road.

"Where do you live?"

His eyes flicked sideways to mine, amusement glinting there as his mouth kicked up at one corner. My belly did a quick flip in response.

"This way," he teased.

I rolled my eyes. "I gathered as much."

The moon was rising in the sky, illuminating the Green Mountains in the distance. I loved Vermont and the way its rolling hills made you feel like you were cradled within the mountains.

Ty took another turn. While we were only a few minutes outside of downtown Colebury, the houses were spread apart, and I guessed we were close to the countryside. Maybe not in the farmlands of Tuxbury, but definitely on the way there.

His truck bounced down a gravel drive, rolling to a stop in front of a barn illuminated by his headlights. "Do you live in a barn?"

He cut the engine to his truck, glancing over. "I do. But I promise I don't live in the old stalls."

At his slow grin, my belly flipped again. Although uncertainty was still flickering in the back of my thoughts, the funny thing was it felt easy to be with Ty. The fiery chemistry between us burned too hot and reduced my worries to ash.

Another moment later, we were walking inside through a side door. I stopped in the downstairs, which was wide open without a single wall, just the supporting structural posts. I swept my eyes around, as Ty spoke. "I'm renovating this whole space. Pretty soon this will all be livable."

"But where are you sleeping?" I had to ask the obvious question.

He smiled down at me, his hand reaching for mine again. With a gentle tug, he led me to some stairs at one end of the barn near the corner where we'd entered. "Upstairs."

I looked around after we crested the top stair and walked through a door. Following his lead, I shrugged out of my light-weight jacket and hung it on the hooks by the door. The upper floor of the barn had an expansive, airy feel to it. To one side, windows offered a lovely view of the moon over the mountains. Most of the space was open with a kitchen at one end. There was only one door and when my eyes landed on it, Ty commented, "Bathroom."

He opened it, and I peered inside to see a clawfoot bathtub on a raised platform with a rainfall showerhead centered above it and a curtain to be pulled around. The floor was tiled with royal blue interspersed with white square tiles.

"Wow, this is really nice," I offered.

"Thanks. I did all the work myself. A family was selling their old farm and divided off part of it. I got the barn and some land. This way they can afford to keep their orchard and upgrade some of the other things they're working on. The way it's set up I can't divide the land any smaller if I ever sell, which is fine because I don't want to."

"Are you going to be a farmer too?" I teased as we walked back toward the kitchen area.

He shrugged. "I don't imagine I'll try to make it a business, but I might enjoy cultivating the apple trees already on the property. I wouldn't do it for work, more for fun."

Before I could respond, Ty was reeling me close and dipping his head to kiss me again, and it was exactly what I wanted. Because kissing him made me forget everything else.

One of his palms cupped my cheek, his thumb brushing in

slow passes over the wild beat of my pulse in my throat. He angled his head to the side, his tongue claiming my mouth. I wanted to just give myself over to him. My hormones were chanting for it.

I forgot everything but the feel of his muscled body stepping closer as he deepened our kiss. His other hand slid down my spine in a heated pass, and I let out a shameless gasp into his mouth when his palm slid down over the curve of my bottom, giving it a firm squeeze.

When he broke away and lifted his head, I instantly felt bereft, needing his mouth back on mine right away. As if he could read my mind, he said, "Don't worry, sweetheart. I've got you."

I shivered all over, goosebumps prickling my skin and my nipples tightening to an ache. I wasn't all that aware of where we happened to be standing. Hell, I wasn't aware of much other than Ty and the sweet, decadent escape he offered.

He turned, catching my hand in his as it dropped away from the warm spot he created on my bottom. In another second, he was lifting me up onto the handy kitchen island. I could feel the cool tile surface through the fabric of my skirt. I was wearing a fitted V-neck T-shirt with a long gauzy skirt that twirled around my leather ankle boots. It rumpled slightly around my hips when it rose up. He stepped in between my knees, immediately catching my mouth in another devouring kiss before I could start thinking.

Thinking wasn't on the menu. My brain cells had gone up in smoke, and apparently, *I* was on Ty's personal menu. After starting with a breath stealing kiss, his lips blazed a fiery trail along the underside of my jaw before he nipped lightly at my ear lobe. I shivered again, letting out something between a whimper and a giggle.

Dear God. This man nearly undid me. I wasn't much of a giggler. I couldn't remember the last time I felt carefree. Even at the height of my highs, carefree wasn't the feeling that came with it. It was more of a tension-filled sensation.

With Ty's hand sliding around to pull my hips a little closer to the edge of the counter, I sighed when his tongue dragged along my collarbone and one of his hands cupped my breast. Somehow, he had the exact right touch for me. He wasn't all grabby, but firm and confident. With every touch, sensation stormed through me.

I needed to get a good feel of him—a thorough reminder of just how delectable his body was. He let out a little hum of satisfaction when I slid one of my palms up under his shirt to map the planes of his chest, glorying in the warmth of his skin and the dusting of hair there. I could feel the hard press of his arousal at the cradle of my hips.

As before when I was with him, things moved really fast the second our hands were on each other. Everything became a blur of sensation, one touch rolling into the next as the sparks scattered through me.

He yanked my T-shirt off, letting out a growl of satisfaction. I dragged my eyes open to find his dark gaze on me as he ran his tongue along his teeth. He let out something between a growl and a low moan that ended with, "Belle."

Before I could even formulate a reply, he dipped his head and his warm, wet mouth closed over a nipple, right through the black lace of my bra. I cried out at the piercing pleasure that zinged to my core. My pussy clenched, and I felt the slick moisture there. My hips rocked restlessly.

He deftly unhooked my bra, cupping both breasts. He took his time, teasing one nipple and then the other with his lips and teeth. I was incoherent, pressure already tightening inside of me. It had been a while since I'd been with a man and actually had an orgasm. I was no prude, and I even had a favorite vibrator, although I didn't name it. I wasn't *that* ridiculous. No judgment though to those who did. I was needy and desperate for release.

To make matters more desperate, my last few experiences with sex had been a major let down. Yet, I knew the promise of Ty's touch. I yanked at his shirt, gasping, "I need to feel you."

He straightened, hooking a hand behind his head and tugging his T-shirt off in a quick motion. Then, I had the glorious feel of his bare skin against mine. He wasted no time, his palms sliding up my calves, the calloused surface sending hot shivers through me with goosebumps chasing in the wake of his touch.

"This skirt is convenient," he murmured against my lips before he took my mouth in another devouring kiss. One kiss tumbled into another and then another. There were so many kisses, I lost count.

He pushed my knees apart, the fabric of my skirt rumpling around my hips. I was clenching tight for him and so wet, my hips rolled restlessly. He chose now to torture me.

He straightened, his eyes dropping down. I was pretty careless when it came to clothes. I did like a comfortable skirt, but otherwise I usually wore jeans and a T-shirt. My one and only penchant was lingerie. I liked silk and lace because they made me feel sexy.

He murmured something indecipherable and teased his fingers over the damp silk. My hips arched toward him, and I let out a frustrated whimper when he immediately drew away.

He lifted his eyes and rested his hands on the counter on either side of my hips. His gaze was searing and intense, and my belly flipped. I was trying to catch my breath, but I couldn't. It came in short, sharp pants.

"We're almost to the point of no return." His voice was low, the vibration of it thrumming through my body.

"Don't you dare stop," I gasped. As orders went, it was kind of weak with my voice raspy and breathless. But I meant it. I would do him bodily harm at this point if he tried to stop.

Ty's lips curled in one of those slow grins, sending heat in a swift wash through me. Every little thing was fuel poured on the fire of our desire.

"Yes ma'am," was all he said before he dipped his head and caught one of my nipples in his mouth.

I cried out when he gave it a hard suck right when his fingers pushed the silk out of the way between my thighs and teased into my dripping wet folds. I was so close, so frantic for it, that my climax surprised me.

He sank two fingers inside me, knuckle deep, his thumb teasing over my swollen clit. I came hard and fast, trembling as the climax burst through me, pleasure rushing in a fierce wave.

Before I had fully recovered, his mouth was on mine, and we tumbled into another commanding kiss. I reached between us, needing more already, needing him.

I fumbled to get his jeans unbuttoned, letting out a sigh of satisfaction when I slipped my hand in to find his cock hard, the skin velvety and warm under my touch. Ty murmured something on my neck. He was teasing me on that sensitive skin behind my ear, but I was undeterred, rolling my thumb over the tip and swiping a drop of pre-cum.

Just when I thought I was going to get to take charge, he lifted me, carrying me swiftly across the room and around behind the screen at the other end of the barn. Next thing I knew, he was stretching me out on a bed. I kicked my boots off over the side of the bed and heard the thump of his shoes following. He shucked his jeans and boxers and produced a condom from somewhere, rolling it on swiftly.

"Hurry," I demanded.

Ty chuckled as his knee pressed on the mattress between my thighs, and his weight came over me. Oh God. He felt so good, every inch of him was muscle. And he was warm, so warm.

When I felt his cock between my thighs, the pressure of his thick crown right at my slick entrance, he paused, brushing my tangled hair away from my face. His elbows were resting by my shoulders.

"Are you—" he began

I cut him off. "I'm absolutely sure."

Curling my legs around his hips, I drew him closer, and he filled me in one swift thrust. I cried out. He held still for several beats of my heart, and, in all honesty, I needed a moment to adjust. Ty wasn't just tall and broad shouldered, he was big all over, and he filled me thoroughly.

After a moment, he drew back, filling me again in increments, and I moaned at the delicious stretch. He settled into a rhythm, a smooth pull and glide, sending pressure spiraling inside me again, cinching more tightly with every stroke. His skin was damp against mine.

My skirt was bunched at my waist, and I didn't even care. With each stroke, I rose to meet him, the wave curling tighter and tighter inside me until he thrust into me one more time, slow and deep, just as he reached between us and did something magic with his fingers. The pleasure burst, raying through my body like liquid fire as my channel rippled around him. I didn't even know how it was possible, but this climax was more intense than the first.

He buried himself inside me once more, letting out a rough cry before he bowed his head, shuddering in the embrace of my legs. After a moment, he eased to my side. His hand moved in a slow pass over my belly before he drew out and rested beside me.

It was all over but for our ragged breathing. It felt as if I was coming down from a crazy high, two earth shattering climaxes leaving me replete. His thumb traced in a lazy circle around my belly button, and I rolled my head to the side. His eyes were closed, but his lashes swept up the moment I looked his way. The second I met his heavy-lidded gaze, I felt a deep pull in the center of my chest, and a tug low in my belly.

Belle's wide brown eyes held mine, and I wanted to lean over and kiss the freckles on her cheeks. Uncertainty flickered in her gaze, but it passed quickly. She surprised me by lifting her hand and smoothing a fingertip over one of my eyebrows. Her lips curled in a small smile as her hand fell to rest on my chest. "It was messy," she explained.

"My eyebrow?"

She nodded, blinking as her cheeks went a little pink.

"Well, thank you then," I offered somberly.

She bit her lip and laughed. I took the moment to let my eyes absorb the sight of her. With her flushed skin, her bright eyes, and her swollen lips, she was disarmingly delectable. Hell, I could've gone another round right then. I hadn't been living as a monk, but I also hadn't exactly found much time of late for women, much less women who got to me the way Belle did.

If I was being honest with myself, no woman got to me like Belle. She was singular in her ability to set me on fire. We were just *that* good together. It was easy and fucking hot.

Just then, I noticed she was still wearing her skirt. I chuckled, and she asked, "What's so funny?"

"We never got your skirt off."

She grinned, and a sly look entered her eyes. "Maybe not, but at least I got my panties and boots off."

I laughed, and she traced circles on my chest with a fingertip. I lifted a palm, needing to touch her. I smoothed it over the sweet curve of her shoulder, my eyes landing on the tattoo at the top of her shoulder blade. With her angled toward me, it was just visible. "This is new." It was a heart, drawn as if carved into wood, the lines of the grain etched in varying subtle shades of brown and gold. "It's beautiful," I added.

"How do you know it's new?" Her big brown eyes lifted to mine, a saucy hint contained there.

"Because I would remember if you had it before. I didn't forget anything about you." The moment I said that, my heart gave a tricky kick. Belle had this way of sliding right through my defenses. I revealed perhaps too much with that comment.

She blinked as a wash of pink bloomed on her cheeks. She swallowed, her lashes sweeping down again. "I didn't have it before. My father's a woodcarver in his spare time. I always loved watching him on the weekends when I was little." Her lashes lifted again, vulnerability flickering in her gaze for a flash. "It's to represent heartwood. That's the densest and strongest part of the tree."

I absorbed that as I traced the edges of the heart with my fingertip. "It's beautiful," I repeated.

Quiet spun out between us. She dipped her head, nipping lightly on my shoulder. I shifted closer and laid another kiss on her, for no other reason than that I loved kissing Belle. She had a sassy tongue, and she never hesitated to throw herself into kisses.

When I drew back, she asked, "Is this when I find a way to gracefully depart?"

"Hell, no. I've got you for the whole night."

Her throaty laugh rang out, and I pulled her on top of me, kissing her again because I wanted her, and I wanted to dive into her fire. I wasn't so sure I wanted to think too hard about just how fiercely I wanted her to stay.

"You're going where?" Belle asked.

She was standing just outside the doorway that led to the stairs. Her cheeks were pink, and her hair was damp. I wanted to drag her back to bed and stay there all day. But I actually had somewhere to be, and apparently, she needed to get into Speakeasy for a morning meeting with the kitchen staff. Seeing as I had driven her out here with me last night, I was her ride back to town.

"I'm going to help my sister. She needs a little help with some shelving in her new place," I explained.

"Oh, where does your sister live?" she asked as I held the door open and we walked through together. I didn't bother locking it behind me. Break-ins weren't something people worried about all that much in Vermont.

"Burlington. She's getting her Master's there. She's ecstatic to be living on her own."

"How old is she?"

Belle gave me a little eye roll when I held the door to my truck open for her. I shrugged. "I have manners."

She hopped in quickly, and I rounded the truck, answering her question once I was in the driver's seat. "Jess is twenty-two. She attended college near where we grew up, so she stayed at home then. My mom worries about her a lot."

"The usual worry, or something extra?" Belle asked.

"Something extra. She was burned in a car accident when she was little. Nobody died, but the car caught fire." I started the truck and headed out my driveway. "Anyway, she was in the back and got burned." Pausing, I shook my head. "The guy who caused the accident was driving drunk. He'd gotten out of a prior DUI due to a technicality, and he'd stolen the car he was driving. He never should've even been driving, but it changed my sister's life permanently."

Belle gasped, and when I glanced her way, she looked horri-fied. "She's okay, I swear," I offered.

Belle nodded jerkily, and I continued. "Jess almost died from infections from the burns and was in and out of the hospital for a bit. My mom was crazy protective for years. Long story short, I'm going to go help Jess put some shelving up. She's too fucking stubborn to ask anybody else for help."

When I stopped at the end of my drive and glanced to Belle, her eyes were still wide. "You are a good brother," she said.

"I try."

A few minutes later, I dropped Belle off. When she looked across the seat at me, I had the urge to kiss her. But she moved swiftly, unbuckling her seatbelt and hopping out. When she looked my way again, her cheeks went a little pink. "Thanks for the ride."

We stared at each other, and the air felt heavy for a few seconds. "Anytime."

After she hurried up the stairs to her apartment, I aimed for the highway.

14

TY

Hands on hips, I stared down at the shelving parts Jess had ordered online. "All right, we can have this together pretty quick."

My sister snorted from where she stood a few feet away. I glanced up, my lips tugging into a grin. "What?" I prompted.

She pointed to the side of her neck and then mine. I raised a brow in question because I had no clue what she meant.

"You have a hickey."

I rolled my eyes. "So, what if I do?"

"Who's the lucky girl?" Jess asked, lobbing a question right back at me.

I opened my mouth to say something cutting or dismissive, but then I shrugged. "Nobody you know."

There was no sense in pretending like there wasn't a hickey on my neck. I didn't doubt there was, it's just I'd barely even looked in the mirror this morning. And *that* was because I'd been feeling utterly satisfied after teasing Belle to another climax in the shower. Among other details I recalled about Belle, she was a generous girl. She'd returned the favor and worked magic with her mouth on my cock.

I wasn't planning to discuss *any* of this with my little sister.

"Do you like her?" Jess asked as I leaned over and began separating out the pieces of shelving.

I glanced up quickly. "I do." My answer surprised me. Not because I didn't know if I liked Belle, but because I said so aloud. But then, if there was one person I tended to share anything personal with, it was my sister.

Jess took a step, easing her hips to the floor. The burns she'd sustained when she was a little girl had been bad enough that one of her legs was permanently stiff. The skin was tight and deeply scarred around her knee. When she was younger, amidst the various surgeries they had done and in the aftermath of infections, she'd used a brace for a while. She often eschewed using any support as she'd gotten older. She chose to limp around, telling me she preferred that to the looks she got when she wore her brace, although she still used it sometimes.

I sat cross legged on the floor, glancing over at her. We shared the same coloring, although her hair was straighter and a shade darker than mine. Her eyes held mine as she waited patiently for me to offer more information. "What's she like? And, how long have you known her?" she pressed.

I did some quick math in my head. I was now twenty-nine, and I'd been a senior at twenty-two when I met Belle. "More than seven years," I offered.

"What?!" Jess reached up to adjust her ponytail, tightening it before her hands fell to her lap.

I chuckled. "I knew her in my senior year at college. Haven't seen her since then. But she took a job as a chef at Speakeasy."

"Oh. So, were you guys hot and heavy before? It's not like you would've told me."

My sister was seven years younger than me, so I definitely wouldn't have been chatting about my sex life with her. Then, or now. "Toss me that bag over there." I gestured to the prepared bag of parts for the shelving.

Jess tossed it over and I opened it, quickly sorting the various pieces. I began assembling the frame for the shelf as I answered,

"If you're asking if we were serious then, no. But, I did really like her."

"How long have you been seeing her since she started working at Speakeasy?"

"Geez, Jess, you're seriously grilling me."

"Well, you're my favorite brother. If you're getting serious with someone, I need to meet her."

I chuckled. "We haven't been seeing each other long," I offered, avoiding the detail that we'd only had one night together since Belle reappeared in my life. Not because I needed to keep that secret, but because it startled me to realize how much I wanted us to be more than a fling. "We're not serious yet, and I'm your only brother, so no sense in playing the favorites card," I added.

Jess shrugged nonchalantly. "Yeah, but we could hate each other, and we don't."

I grinned over at her. "Very true. You're my favorite sister."

"I'd better be," she said firmly. "Now, what else do we need?"

I helped Jess get the shelves done and ran a few errands with her. Just as I was leaving around noon, she caught me lightly by the elbow. "Don't be afraid to give this girl a chance."

I stared at her blankly. Her lips pressed in a line, and she let out a quick sigh. "You know what I mean. We have shitty role models in our parents as far as relationships go. Hell, I'm still waiting for the day that we find out Dad has a secret family that we didn't even know about."

I let out a dry laugh. "Do you mean in addition to his decades-long affair with Cheryl?"

Jess's ponytail bounced with her firm nod. "Totally. I'm hoping now that I finally moved out, maybe Mom will get a clue and leave him." Her eyes narrowed as she looked at me and cocked her head to the side. "You know what I mean. You are the master at keeping your distance."

My chest tightened a little because I knew exactly what she meant. Maybe Belle shined brightly in my memories as far as hookups went, but that's why it had been no trouble to let her be nothing more than that back then. Keeping people at a distance came easily to me.

I looked back at my sister and shrugged. "Maybe so. I could say the same about you."

Jess cuffed me lightly on the shoulder before leaning forward and giving me a quick hug. Stepping back, she said, "Thanks for your help. Call me."

I drove away, my mind churning over Jess's uncomfortably accurate observation. The thing was, it was easy to keep people at a distance because our parents' marriage was fucking shit. Beyond the fact our father was an asshole, Jess's accident had given my mother something to throw herself into. She ignored the wasteland of her marriage and my fathers' years long infidelity with another woman.

My mother had been utterly occupied with Jess. My memories weren't all that clear of exactly how long Jess was in the hospital after the initial accident, but I'd understood it was serious. I remembered my mom being gone most of the time while I was alone in the house a lot. My dad was there occasionally and barely paid attention to me. Our interactions were limited to him snapping at me if I left a mess anywhere. Boys weren't exactly legendary for being tidy and clean, so that was fun.

After the initial scare for my sister, there were other surgeries as they tried to repair her leg. All in all, the time added up. By the time I reached high school, it felt like I'd been functioning mostly on my own. The one and only bright spot was Jess and I had each other. Somehow, we fostered a strong bond when she was home more and constantly chafing at my mother's heavy worry and sarcastically calling out my dad's absence.

Hockey had been my escape and I'd been damn good at it, which was a blessing. Being that competitive at the sport absorbed all of my spare time. Parents usually had to be absorbed as well. The one thing my father did was take me to practice. We would ride in silence in the car. My mother's contribution had been to rustle up carpools to games and practices with various friends when needed.

When I had to accept the bitter pill of my knee injury sidelining my hopes for a pro career, I'd known two things: I didn't want to work for my father, and I knew I wanted to find a place where I could create my own life, preferably someplace where people didn't worry about things like money and superficial success.

It was a blessing to have my sister move to Vermont as well. She was the only person I was close with in my family. I loved my mom, but we weren't tight.

My thoughts spun back to Jess's comment that I was a master at keeping my distance. I knew she was right, and I wasn't sure how I felt about that.

Belle tugged at me. Whether she meant to or not, little hooks had caught on the binding around my heart, loosening and unraveling it. She was leading me to an unfamiliar place, one where perhaps I wanted more.

When I got back to Colebury, I aimed for Speakeasy. The moment I parked my truck, anticipation sizzled through my veins. Because I knew Belle was here. Even if she was working, just as I would be in a few minutes, knowing she would be near had anticipation humming in my veins.

A few minutes later, I was in the brewing room checking on a few things. Alec and Griffin were bantering about beer and cider, a favorite topic for them.

"We don't have to worry about Goldenpour stock here," Griffin was saying.

Alec nodded enthusiastically at this. "And, your cider's getting a reputation."

Griffin rubbed his hand over his beard. Griffin was a big guy, more brains than brawn. The guy actually had a degree in chemistry. Like me, he'd played sports in college, football in his case. Every so often we chatted about our former sports lives. He was as philosophical as I was, and lately, he was also damned happy. He had a girl he loved and a kid. Plus, brewing was a serious passion for him. The guy would happily chat about the nitty-gritty details for hours.

"You planning on expanding your cider operation?" I asked. Griffin's cider was a favorite at Speakeasy.

"As soon as I can make it work, money-wise," Griffin replied.

"Making award-winning cider should help solve that problem sooner rather than later," I offered. Griffin grinned at that. I glanced at my watch. "I gotta get up front, guys."

Just then, Audrey appeared with her and Griffin's toddler on her hip. The second Griffin saw them, a smile broke across his face.

"Good to see you Audrey," I said with a wave as I passed her by.

She gave me a smile. "We have your favorite muffins today," she called.

"Pear ginger?" I asked as I stopped briefly in the doorway.

"Of course!" she replied.

"I'll stop by and get some if I have time."

I hurried up front, immediately getting swept into the busy afternoon. Lily was raking in the tips for us at the bar. I only got a few glances of Belle as the afternoon rolled into evening. There was a local wedding at a nearby family farm, and it brought in plenty of people looking for the best beer around and Colebury's newest restaurant.

Phoebe's grand opening had been a smash, and we were continuing to build on that. I was in the middle of restocking some beer when I heard Belle's voice. "Oh, I didn't know you guys were coming tonight."

Glancing beyond the bar, I was surprised to see her in the restaurant. She still had on her chef's jacket. She was standing beside an older couple. With a quick glance, I deduced they must be her parents. The woman looked quite a bit like Belle, although her dark hair was streaked with silver.

"It's okay, dear," she was saying as she patted Belle on the shoulder. "We just wanted to get some dinner."

Lily, bless her charming heart, stopped beside them as she was returning to the bar from checking on something. "We've got an open table right now," she whispered to Belle.

Belle looked distracted and worried. She happened to catch my eyes. I got the sense she felt a little out of sorts and vulnerable, and I experienced a twinge in my chest. I wanted to tell her it was all going to be okay, and I had no idea what she was distressed about. There was nothing I could do though. The restaurant was hopping.

It was one thing to want Belle. That was easy, as easy as breathing for me. But this other feeling—wanting to protect her, to comfort her—was entirely unfamiliar. I felt as if I'd been dropped in the middle of nowhere without a map to help me find my way.

15

BELLE

I zipped through the motions of getting a dish ready before checking with the line cooks about a confusing order that had been sent back by a table.

Phoebe appeared at my shoulder. "You know, you're done for the night."

Glancing up, I shrugged. "We're still really busy. I can stay a little late."

Phoebe held my eyes for a long beat. "Your parents are here for dinner, right?"

I focused, rather intently, on making a pretty display of raspberry sauce on a cheesecake dessert special. "Uh-huh."

"Why don't you go eat with them?" Phoebe pressed.

When I looked up toward her, the anxiety on my face must've given me away. "Oh," Phoebe said softly. "No need to explain. We can always use you for a little extra time."

She hurried off, and blessedly, the restaurant stayed busy. I knew when my parents' order came through, because the waitress actually put "Belle's mom and dad" on the order.

Although Phoebe probably understood the broad strokes of my reticence to have dinner with my parents, my emotions were all tangled up about it. I loved my parents. I even actually liked them. Not everyone could say that about their parents, and I knew I was blessed.

It's just the last few years had created a chasm between us, one that had twists and turns and narrowed and expanded at points. It was only after I had to face them the morning after I'd spent the night in a psychiatric hospital that I learned my mother had a sister with Bipolar Disorder. Somehow, no one saw fit to tell me that before.

I was still a little disgruntled about that detail, although I was even more vexed at the knowledge that no one had paid attention to what that might mean for me. Before I ended up in a full-blown manic phase, I felt like an engine that was running a little too hot all the time. Also, I felt freaking awesome—confident, on top of life, funny, outgoing, and also able to get a shit ton of stuff done. While other people complained about being tired and running out of energy when they were juggling school and work and life, I thought somehow I had a special magic engine that just kept on chugging.

If someone could've warned me maybe I was hypomanic—which I now understood thanks to my therapist and psychiatrist—I might've listened. My mother stayed in touch with my aunt, but she'd moved out to California years ago so she didn't see her too often.

My parents had reached out to her about what happened with me, and she'd been kind enough to call. My shame around everything that happened made it hard, just plain *hard*, to be around my family. I'd let them down so thoroughly. Or, so I believed. That was something my therapist was trying her best to talk me out of.

I was also still smarting from my last stupid relationship. Eric had been brilliant and kind of boring in bed, to be honest. He'd also been "lightly abusive", as I said to my therapist. My parents had been horrified to overhear him shouting belittling comments at me when they happened to stop by for a visit once. I was still grateful he'd ghosted me completely after the mess I made. He was in law school with me and wanted nothing to do with me after that. Thank God. Bad judgment was a fun side effect that came along with my mania.

My efforts to try to repair my image with my parents kept falling short, even though they kept telling me there was nothing to repair and that they loved me exactly how I was. That was hard to square with how they'd always been so proud of my honors status and getting scholarships. All of it had felt awesome, until it wasn't. My life had blown up in my face, and I was still scrambling to find my footing again.

The shining spot was when I was trying to get my shit together and living at home again with them, I figured I might as well get a job as a cook because I loved to cook. Lucking into that chef position at a sweet place in Burlington had given me confidence that I could actually do something other than be a lawyer. It was definitely more fun.

A line cook spun a plate toward me, calling my name as he did and effectively snapping me out of my meandering train of thought. One of the waitresses, Melanie, paused by the end of the stainless-steel counter where I was working. "Your parents are ordering dessert, and they're really taking their time. I think they're hoping you'll come out for a little while."

She smiled when I looked over. I knew she meant well. I managed a brave smile in return. "I'll finish up and join them for dessert."

"They'll love that." She hurried off.

I finished up and finally headed out of the kitchen. I stopped in the staff room to shrug out of my chef's jacket and remove my totally unsexy hairnet. I even went to the restroom to splash water on my face and brush my hair out. After I dabbed my face dry with a stiff paper towel, I paused and stared at my reflection in the mirror.

My cheeks were a little pink from the cold water, making my freckles stand out more than usual. My brown eyes looked right back at me. I wished I knew how to reconcile this girl, the one who didn't feel so confident anymore, with the girl I used to be. I supposed that girl was still somewhere in me. I could still be funny. It's just I felt a little itchy in my skin sometimes, and I hated the uncertainty that dogged me ever since my life had skidded off the tracks.

I idly noticed that my purple streaks were fading a bit, so I would do them this weekend. It would be fun. I snorted to myself. I didn't have the most eventful social life these days. My mind bounced to Ty, like a car bouncing off a railing too fast on the highway and zooming away. I wasn't quite ready to think too hard about Ty and just how deliciously good it felt to be with him.

I could've chalked it up to the hot sexy times, which were definitely incredible, but there was something else to it. Something *more*.

My thoughts around him were even more tangled after learning about his sister's accident and that someone who'd stolen a car caused it. What were the freaking chances of that? My guilt felt like a riptide pulling me under sometimes.

I thought about stuff all the time now. I used to be too busy to think, just zipping from one thing to the other, both in action and thought.

"Get over it," I murmured to myself.

Restless and impatient with myself, I spun away and raced out of the bathroom, promptly colliding with someone. Someone solid and tall and with a great chest. I knew this because my palm landed smack over one of those pecs. I knew before I even looked up it was Ty. Because I could smell him. I didn't know what soap he used, but I liked it. It had a whiff of citrus that mingled with the subtle woodsy scent he carried.

I found his intent gray eyes waiting for me when I lifted my head. "Sorry," I said, so breathlessly I was embarrassed.

Meanwhile, my hormones let out their usual cheer for Ty. They were kind of noisy about the whole thing actually, and I felt a little crazy, as if my hormones were somehow independent of me. Nobody ever said hormones were smart.

"No worries," Ty said with one of his quick, easy grins. His eyes crinkled at the corners, and my belly did a little twist and spin.

I hurried past him, feeling foolish. I needed to be casual. It was just sex. Hookups had been easy for me before, no big thing. Even if Ty held a memorable place because of how high the flames flickered with him, I'd been able to manage it.

A moment later, I slipped into the empty chair at my parents' table. "Hey, Mom. Hey, Dad."

My mother leaned over and kissed me on the cheek quickly, and my father squeezed my shoulder and dipped his head with a warm smile.

My mother had big brown eyes like me, and rather than purple streaks in her hair, she had natural silver. Tonight, she had twisted her hair up into a bun with two chopsticks stabbed through it. She was dressed in her usual style, what I referred to as hippie-elegant. She wore a bright blue skirt, with a flowing cream-colored blouse. My father's hair was all silver, and he had blue eyes and a kind smile. It kind of amused me that they were both lawyers.

What I thought I had always wanted to be. I ignored that little pinch of confusion and smiled between them. "How was dinner?"

"Absolutely delicious. We've heard nothing but rave reviews about this place. People are even talking about it in Burlington."

"Seriously?" I asked.

My father nodded. "Of course. With Giltmaker Brewery associated with it, word travels. They *do* make the most popular beer in Vermont. Plus, you know how the restaurants are in New England. People love hearing about those out of the way places in smaller towns. They're special."

"And we're so proud of your work here," my mother chimed in.

See, now this drove me slightly insane. They were worried about me feeling like I'd let them down, because I made the mistake of telling them I worried about that. So now, they were constantly trying to tell me how proud they were of my cooking.

"I know you are, Mom. How are things at home?" My voice was bright, a little too bright.

"Busy as usual. The fall semester's picking up, and your father's practice is always busy."

"Well, that's good. Neither one of you likes to have time on your hands. I know this because I inherited that tendency."

My father chuckled, and my mother smiled, and we actually managed to get through that tense part of our conversation. Matters were helped by Lily. She chatted when she stopped at the table as she passed by in between slinging drinks at the bar. "Did you try the Honey Bear Bourbon?" she asked my mother. "It's delicious."

There was a reason Lily had a reputation for getting the most tips behind the bar. She was just one of those people who was easy to be around. No conversation ever felt forced with her, and she could even make bad weather sound charming.

When my mother glanced to me, I nodded encouragingly. "You should try it. Not only is it good, but it's from an all-female brewery."

I walked my parents out to the parking lot afterwards. "Where is your car?" my mother asked, her eyes arcing about the parking lot.

"Mom, I told you, I live right down the street. I walk to work. It's good for me, and I love walking."

"Well, now when winter—"

My father cut in. "Belle's been driving on winter roads since she learned how to drive, Marsha."

My mother pursed her lips, casting a sheepish smile at me. "Sorry. You know I worry."

"You can worry, but I'm doing great. I promise."

We'd gotten past my mother's urge to ask if I was taking my medication. I had a full year of living with them after my little stint in the hospital. I had to remind myself time and again it had only been one night. But that night lived large in my memory, and that of my parents.

"'Night, Mom." I gave them quick hugs and watched as they drove away.

I was stuffing my hands in my pockets when I heard a voice call over, "Good job with the 'rents, Belle."

Spinning around, I saw May Shipley sitting on the bench by the employee entrance. I kicked a pebble with the toe of my boot as I walked over to her. "Ya think?" I teased as I sat down beside her.

May smiled over at me. "If there's one thing I understand, it's families who worry about you. Mine lives here," she said dryly.

I laughed softly. "Right, so you've said. You seem like you've got your shit together these days. Hell, at least you graduated from law school."

May gave me a stern look. "You know you can go back to school and finish if you want. I didn't think that's what you wanted."

I took a deep breath, letting it out and feeling the tension ease slightly in my chest as I did. "I don't think I do. It's just I was such a good girl. I did everything right, until I did everything *really* wrong."

May scooted closer to me and curled her arm around my shoulders, giving me a little squeeze before shifting back again. "We all have to screw up. At least, that's what they tell me when I go to my AA meetings. Trust me, if you want to hear some stories that'll make you feel a little better, come with me to a meeting. I feel like an underachiever when I'm there sometimes. Then, I feel guilty about that because I don't mean that in a judgy way."

I laughed. "I get it."

"Seriously though, if you really want to reconsider law school, you know you could. But rumor has it, people love your food here, so you'll probably get more accolades doing this than going the law route."

I thought about how close I'd been to graduating from law school. I thought a little more about what it might feel like to try to go back. For now, I couldn't dredge up the motivation.

Glancing sideways to catch May's gaze again, I asked, "You've heard about my food?"

She gave me a pointed look. "Yes. Phoebe got things off with a bang, and I've heard your specials are awesome."

Just then, the door near the bench opened and my head swiveled along with May's to see who was coming out. The second my eyes landed on Ty's broad shoulders, my pulse took off at a fast gallop and heat sizzled down my spine. Ty hadn't even looked our way yet, and here I was, getting all hot and bothered.

"Hey Ty, you happen to know when Alec will be out?" May called.

Ty held a garbage bag that looked to be filled with bottles in one hand and turned to glance our way. He cast May one of his easy grins, before his eyes shifted to me. His gaze lingered just long enough for heat to suffuse me. I was relieved for the almost darkness and the cool autumn night air.

"I imagine he'll be out in a few minutes," Ty replied when his eyes flicked back to May.

She drummed her fingertips on the railing of the bench. "Looks busy tonight."

"It's busy every night," Ty replied with a chuckle. "Speaking of, I need to get back in there."

With a wink that I knew wasn't meant specifically for me and another grin, he crossed the parking lot and tossed the bag in the recycling bin. A moment later, he had returned inside. The sounds of the busy kitchen and bar briefly filtered to the parking lot when he opened the door before it was muted as it closed.

May glanced my way, giving me a curious look. "Well, that was hot."

I didn't see how she could have any idea just how *hot* I literally was from nothing more than a passing interaction with Ty. "What?" I asked, my voice coming out a little squeaky and raspy at the same time.

"That look he gave you. Totally hot. So, tell me, have you

given in and had a little fun yet?"

I wanted to lie and deny it, but I didn't really have anyone to talk to these days. I was still settling into this small town and finding my way. I could really use a friend. Finding my way applied to more than this town. I felt my cheeks get hotter again as I tried to reply nonchalantly, "Maybe."

May chuckled. "Good for you. You need to have fun. We all do sometimes."

My blush faded quickly, and I let out a sigh. "I know. It's just that fun used to get me in trouble."

"You're not going to get in trouble. When Alec and I first got together, it was all about the fun, and nothing went wrong."

Panic tightened in my chest, and I felt my eyes go wide as I stared at her. "Right, and now you two are living together and probably planning to get married and have kids. I don't think I'm ready to go there."

May wrinkled her nose, eyeing me warmly. "It's okay, Belle. You can just have fun. Plus, Ty is a really nice guy. Who's to say it couldn't be more than that?"

"Would you please stop? I can't think past trying to have a little fun. Anything else is too complicated."

"Okay." She was all easy and breezy. "Was it good?" she teased, leaning closer.

I punched her lightly on the shoulder. "Stop it. And yes, of course it was."

As if he somehow knew I needed to be rescued from this conversation, Alec came out the back door then. He was a tall, handsome guy. He cast a friendly smile at me. Of course, he was already holding his hand out and tugging May up from the bench. Alec had no problem with PDA and seemed to like to have May close to him whenever she happened to be in his vicinity.

"Sorry I'm late," he murmured as he pressed a lingering kiss on her cheek.

I actually flushed a little as she looked up at him. The intimacy between them was so clear, it felt as if I were interrupting.

May smiled at him. "No worries. I was hanging out with Belle."

"Those spicy wings you made for a special this week were freaking awesome," Alec offered as he glanced my way again.

"I aim to please," I said as I stood.

"Coffee again soon?" May asked as she laced her fingers with Alec's.

"Any time before noon. Just text me. I'm always up early."

I watched as they walked away, aiming for the trees between Speakeasy and The Gin Mill. They walked to the very path that led to the bench where I first kissed Ty. I doubted they were planning to stop at the bench and make out. Alec and May lived in an apartment on the third floor above The Gin Mill, they didn't need to make do with public benches.

I experienced a burn in my chest, wishing I had someone to share my life with. *That* startled the hell out of me.

Of late, all I wanted was to find a small island of stability, a place where I knew I would be okay. I didn't want to feel lonely, and lately, that's exactly how I felt. I didn't have my sparkling confidence to carry me. No more honors student, no more shooting star into a law career that I wasn't even sure I'd ever wanted.

I walked across the parking lot, turning onto the sidewalk and crossing the street to the town green to make my way up the hill to my little apartment. I thought about how it felt to fall asleep with Ty the other night. Longing pierced me. I wished he were here with me tonight. And, not just for the sexy times, although those sure were great. Rather, I craved his presence and how easy it was to be with him.

That was crazy thinking. I needed to get my shit together, not tumble into a relationship. Not to mention that I doubted Ty viewed me as relationship material. Especially not since I told him the truth. Who wanted to be with a girl who skidded off course as spectacularly as I had? Ty didn't even know all of the ugly details. In particular, that I'd stolen a car.

BELLE

My therapist cocked her head to the side, tapping her fingers lightly on the arm of her chair. Laura had big blue eyes behind round glasses and paired with curly gray hair. She gave off this aging hippie vibe. Today, she was wearing sandals with wool socks. Totally not trendy, but it suited her perfectly, along with her lightweight cargo pants and practical blouse, which I was positive was made of that fabric that didn't wrinkle, which was kind of weird and miraculous.

"Belle, there are people all over the world who have relationships, marriages, and families with people who have the very same diagnosis you do. Bipolar Disorder is not some kind of life sentence. In fact, I'd be willing to bet you have no idea how many people around you are dealing with their own challenges."

Laura said this in her usual calm tone, however it was laced with a hint of exasperation. She'd met me the week after my night at the hospital. After a year of knowing me, she didn't hesitate to share her opinion when she thought I was giving myself too hard of a time.

"But—" I began, immediately stopping to gather my thoughts. "I know everyone's dealing with something, it's just..." I sighed.

"I was in a psych hospital for a night. I feel like most people would think that was, well, a lot."

"It was one night, and you were in a manic phase. The chemical situation in your brain was *not* good during that time. Actually, you totally get a pass," she said, lifting her hand and waving it casually in the air.

I glared at her. "I get a pass?"

"Not really," she said with a little laugh. "Bipolar Disorder is a chemical state in your brain. When you're having a manic phase, things are out of whack, chemically speaking. You've been on medication and managed it well for over a year. As we've discussed, it's something you need to be aware of and continue to manage. Do I need to remind you of all the famous people who have Bipolar Disorder? Or, shall I reel off statistics associated with various mental health issues? You are not alone, and you are not crazy."

"I know, I know." I leaned my face into my hands, my breath filtering through my fingers with my sigh before I lifted my head up again and brushed my hair away from my face. "I don't want to have a full-blown manic phase ever again, but I wouldn't mind having just a little bit of it." I held up my thumb and forefinger with a tiny gap between them. "Just enough so I can feel that little hit of confidence." I shook my head. "That doesn't really make any sense."

Laura tilted her head to the side, her eyes warm and understanding. "Right, but it wasn't based on genuine confidence. You're struggling with this realignment in your life, which is completely expected. It would be weird if you weren't. You're still brilliant, but you were floating along doing everything you thought your parents wanted. Maybe that *is* what you actually want, but I don't know that *you* know that yet. Before you go thinking this is something only you would struggle with and beating yourself up about that, just stop that right now. Frankly some people have what's described as a midlife crisis because they do what they think they should do all the way up until they get old enough to wonder if maybe they chose the wrong path. In a strange way, your manic episode has forced you to reconsider your choices much sooner. Maybe you will go back to law school. Maybe not."

My head was shaking all on its own, and Laura smiled softly. "See, you *do* know, or I think you do. You need to figure out how to feel good on your own, so you can make decisions about what you want without the external accolades buoying you."

"What do you mean?" I pressed, a sneaky sense of uncertainty unspooling inside.

"Getting honors, scholarships, having your friends look up to you, and thinking law school was what you wanted because you thought it was what your parents wanted for you. Having met your parents, I think they want whatever makes you happy. Like most parents, they reinforce what you do well, and you're a pleaser so you did what they thought you wanted. In turn, they praised you for that, and the cycle turned into a nice little merry-go-round that wasn't helpful."

We'd had several variations of this conversation. I bit my lip, contemplating something I wasn't sure I was ready to tell her but thought I probably should.

"I had sex," I announced, rather forcefully.

Ever unflappable, Laura simply nodded. "I hope it was what you wanted. I also hope it was good." Her lips quirked at that.

My cheeks got hot. "It was, but I think maybe it was a mistake."

"How come? There's nothing wrong with having fun. I've been pointing that out for a while now. I'm a little concerned that you think you can never have fun again."

I rolled my eyes. "I don't think that. I'm just trying to figure out how to do life."

"Tell me about the person you were with."

"He was a guy I knew before. He was a college hockey star, and we had a few hookups back in the day."

Laura nodded, waiting for me to add more information, like she always did. Sometimes, I found her patience annoying.

"It was great, and he's a good guy. I made the mistake of telling him about my situation," I said, flapping my hand vaguely in the air.

"Was this before or after your latest encounter?"

"Before. I can't imagine he would consider me relationship material. Not that that's what I'm looking for." I felt pressed to clarify.

Laura regarded me, warmth and understanding practically radiating like beams from her eyes. "Why do you think you can't have a relationship? I mean that seriously."

"Because who would want to have a relationship with me?" I pressed my hands to my eyes and then flung them away.

"Belle, you are a bright, kind, funny woman. Obviously, I'm your therapist, but I've spent enough time with you to know that plenty of people would want to have a relationship with someone like you."

"But I'm really a mess," I said quietly.

Laura shrugged, all nonchalant, like my mistakes were totally no big deal. "You're not any more of a mess than most of the world. You just think you are and that's the problem. You have your symptoms managed. I think it's great you had sex. And if it's good, I think you should have more." It was almost funny that my therapist wanted to make sure the sex was good. She paused before adding, "I hope he's not abusive like your last boyfriend."

I shook my head quickly. "No. He's not like that at all. What should I do?"

"You want me to tell you what to do?"

"Well, I don't know what to do. Is it okay that I don't know what to do? What if he just wants to fool around and I end up wanting more? Or what if he wants more, and I don't?" My questions tumbled out swiftly.

Laura nodded solemnly. "These are problems anyone venturing into the possibility of a relationship faces. Obviously, I don't know what he wants. I don't sense that you just want to fool around. That doesn't fit with how you've been approaching life recently."

I took a deep breath as anxiety started to tighten in my chest. I hated when Laura was right, and she so often turned out to be right. It was fucking annoying, really.

This, *this* feeling, it drove me crazy because it was so unlike me. "I hate not knowing what to do," I finally said.

"I know. This feeling is something you're going to have to come to peace with. Uncertainty is part of life, but you can learn to tolerate it. Back to this guy, if he's a nice guy, and you felt comfortable enough to tell him about what's happened in the last year for you, I'm going to guess that means you trust him, at least a little bit."

I nodded. I *did* trust Ty. "He knew me when I was in college and hyper-focused on grades and a little wild, so I kind of felt like I needed to explain why it might seem like I was a little different and why I dropped out of law school."

Laura nodded. "Why don't you consider giving yourself a chance to see what happens? Part of that means you're not going to know what might happen in advance."

I blinked because I felt the tears stinging in my eyes. I wanted more than anything to feel like I was making the right choices in every corner of my life. And I really, *really*, didn't like accepting uncertainty. Even worse, I'd left out something key when I told Ty what happened. The whole stolen car detail, which now felt enormous because of what happened to his sister. I didn't even want to tell Laura, which meant I *had* to tell her.

"I left out something important when I told him what happened," I blurted out.

Ever calm, Laura merely arched a brow.

I sighed. "I didn't tell him I stole a car because I still can't believe I did. It didn't feel like a crime at the time. In the worst coincidence in the world, his sister was badly burned in a car accident when she was little, and the driver who caused the accident was driving a stolen car."

My therapist leaned forward, her words soft and clear. "That's a terrible coincidence, but there's a good chance he'll understand if you tell him the whole truth. If he doesn't, there's nothing you can do about it, but it's not helpful for you to tie yourself in knots over this. You are not some horrible person. You made a mistake during a very difficult time in your life. Everyone screws up. *Everyone.*"

I swallowed, trying to breathe through the tightness in my throat and chest and trying to believe it might be okay with Ty if I told him everything.

"Just do me one favor," Laura said gently.

"What?"

"Don't be so hard on yourself. It's okay not to know, and it's okay to let yourself have something good. I'm actually really proud of you for having sex." She straightened her shoulders and nodded at this.

"You're proud of me?"

"Yes. Especially if it was good. That means you let your guard down."

"You know, you're kind of crazy," I said, laughing a little.

Laura chuckled. "No, I'm not. Now, I think we need to meet again next week."

I rolled my eyes, but I slipped my phone out of my purse and pulled up my work schedule. Because I knew she was right.

The following evening, I walked down to the bench by the river after work. I didn't even try not to wish Ty would find me there.

17

TY

My schedule was nuts for a run of several days when we had one, and then another bartender, end up with a stomach bug. It wouldn't do to have staff spreading that crap around the restaurant, so I covered with an assist from Alec. He liked to stop in regularly as it was to check on things with the brewery.

This afternoon was the usual level of busy, and Alec had stopped by for a few hours and was about to leave. We were discussing the bar's beer stock.

"Our selection of beers is—"

"Unparalleled," Alec said with a grin.

I chuckled. Alec was fun to work with.

"All right, you think you're all set now that Lily is here?" he asked.

"Should be all set. Thanks for carrying those kegs forward."

"I help when I can," Alec replied.

"Exactly why I'm glad I work here," I said before turning away to take the drink order from one of the waitresses handling tables on the floor.

Aside from some passing glimpses of Belle, I didn't have time to seek her out for a few days. Although, even a glimpse of her was a good thing. She was clearly in her element in the kitchen.

She was always zipping around and getting excited when the food got rave reviews from customers.

I almost got myself in a little trouble that evening though. I was in the midst of checking on stock for the bar and passing through the kitchen when Belle called over. "Ty!"

Of course, I knew it was her because I knew her voice too well —husky and melodic, it sent a sizzle through my veins. I turned, as if she had a string attached to me, immediately crossing over to stop beside her at a stainless-steel table on one side of the kitchen.

"Yes?"

Her big brown eyes blinked at me. "I need a taste test."

"It's delish," Lily called over as she hurried past us out to the bar.

"Lily says everything is delicious," Belle offered with a smile. "I love that about her because she's so positive, but I need a critical taster."

"You expect me to be more critical?" I teased.

She gave a light shrug. "Just taste it."

Belle lifted a small plate with some kind of pastry on it. I reached for it, popping it in my mouth. Flavor exploded the second my teeth broke the surface of the flaky, buttery pastry. I closed my eyes, letting out a moan.

"Oh, fuck, that is delicious," I said as I opened my eyes.

Pink crested on her cheeks, and her lips curled in a slow smile. "Really?" She bit the plush surface of her bottom lip, and I came *so* fucking close to kissing her right then and there.

Her lips were simply too tempting, lush and full, and I recalled all too clearly how they felt underneath mine.

"Yes, really?" I insisted when I nudged my brain off the kissing track. "What's in there?"

"Brie with cranberries. It's perfect for autumn and the holidays coming up soon."

"Can I have another?"

She immediately handed me one, and I couldn't hold back another moan as I chewed.

Phoebe came into the back of the kitchen, immediately veering in our direction. I wasn't technically Belle's boss, but I was the general manager. I didn't know what Phoebe would think if she knew about the other night between Belle and me.

"What do we have here?" Phoebe asked when she stopped beside Belle.

"I think I'll add this to the specials for next week," Belle said. "They're the pastry bites I'm testing."

"They're amazing," I said as I backed up. It took an effort to make myself do that when what I wanted to do was linger with Belle. Not for any reason other than I savored the feel of being near her.

Fortunately for me, it was always busy at Speakeasy, so it wasn't difficult to stay distracted. That's what we wanted. The place was developing a good reputation. Hours later, by the time the late shift staff arrived, I was ready to go.

I had to force myself not to check to see if Belle was done for the night. I didn't want to be too obvious. Hell, I was trying not to be obvious in my own mind, which was ridiculous. I walked out into the cool darkness, and my feet carried me to the path that led to the bench.

There was no sign of anyone at the bench, so my feet kept on moving, thinking I'd swing by because my truck was parked over in the lot at The Gin Mill. As I approached the parking lot, I saw Alec and May standing outside. Alec's hand was resting on May's lower back. He said something, and she laughed. I was across the parking lot, and somehow, I felt as if I were interrupting an intimate moment between them. They were a good couple, easy and always kind to each other. When I first got to know Alec, I thought he was fun and easygoing because that's exactly how he was. But he was also deeply caring and protective, and it showed whenever he was around May.

They were by the entrance that led up to the apartments above The Gin Mill. I looked away. There was a small part of me that was almost in awe of what they had. My parents' marriage had taught me nothing good about relationships. I'd never really thought I'd want something serious. Lately though, every so often I wondered if that was a possibility for me.

With a mental shake, I drove home, and did some work in the downstairs of the barn. I was trying to design the layout as such that if I chose, I could create a separate apartment down here. I sure as hell didn't need all the space just for me.

Belle feathered along the edges of my thoughts most of the night, as she had pretty much ever since she'd shown up in town. She was sliding through the tiny slats around my heart, slipping like air through the edge of a windowsill.

Another week later, when it seemed both Belle and I had been doing some kind of avoidance dance with each other, my feet carried me down to that bench by the river, and there she was. The moon was high in the sky tonight, glittering through the trees and shimmering on the river as it rolled quietly over the rocks.

I was a little tired, and more than anything, I'd been craving another night with her. When she glanced up as I rounded the end of the bench, she didn't look the least bit surprised to see me.

Her lips curled in a warm smile. "Hey there, you should sit right here." She patted the bench beside her.

I sat down, because it was impossible not to. Belle was smiling, and her eyes were twinkling, and I wanted to kiss her. Her hair was in a messy bun with a few loose locks dangling around her neck and cheeks.

"How's it going?" she asked.

"You ask that as if you haven't seen me almost every day this whole week," I returned, teasing a little.

"Very true, Ty. You're always busy at work."

"As are you."

She gave me another dimpled smile, and my heart gave a tricky little twist in my chest. I was just supposed to want this girl.

I *did* want her, and I wanted her like no one I'd ever wanted because she was the only girl I could never forget. I kept telling myself I wasn't technically her boss. That might have been splitting hairs, but I didn't really care. Not now, not when I was sitting beside her, and she smelled a little bit like sugar.

"What were you baking this afternoon?"

Her doe eyes widened slightly. "How did you know I was baking?"

"You kind of smell like sugar," I said with a light shrug. Dipping my head, I dusted a kiss on the side of her neck because it was all too tempting.

She bit her lip, and I could see the subtle flush bloom on her cheeks when I straightened. I was trying to be sensible, although I was already toeing the edge of not-so-sensible. Much as I wanted to have my way with her right then and there, this was a public place.

She laughed softly. "Actually, I was making these little Russian wedding cookies."

"Sounds fancy."

"It's a fancy way of saying sugar cookies."

I laughed, pleased when she laughed with me. When I looked her way again, her gaze was thoughtful.

"Okay, smart girl, penny for your thoughts?"

"Oh, my God, you used to call me that," she said with a little snort.

"Well, you *are* a smart girl, and back when I knew you before, you were all about the grades."

She caught one of those loose locks of hair along her neck and spun it around her index finger as one of her feet bounced slightly on the gravel underneath the bench.

"I was, wasn't I? Times have changed. I'm not taking any classes, and I don't care whether or not I get an A on anything," she said, almost solemnly.

"You know, grades aren't everything."

Her eyes whipped up to mine. "They're not."

"You don't sound so sure. I promise you, they're not. I mean, passing matters, and a sense of accomplishment is always important. But in the long run, once you're done with school, who asks about grades? I suppose if you're aiming for some kind of academic position, they would matter. But really, at that point, it's how you do the job. Nobody wants to work with the person who's book smart and a total asshole, or with zero common sense."

Belle grinned at me. "Definitely not." She paused again, looking thoughtful. Another spin of that lock of hair around her finger before her hand fell to her lap. "It took me a while to accept the idea of not worrying about grades. I obsessed about them for years."

I cocked my head to the side. "That wasn't how I saw it. You were really driven, but not obsessed. It seemed like good grades came easy to you. Life is harder than classes."

"Well, I definitely figured *that* out." Her tone was dry, and she nudged me lightly with her elbow. "There's no syllabus, so I can't do anything ahead of time, and there's no grading rubric."

"So true. Everyone plays by their own set of rules, and the rules can change."

She smiled at me again, and it felt like a precious gift. I didn't sense Belle revealed her insecurities to many people. Knowing that she could find humor in them meant she was letting her guard down. I liked knowing that.

"What are you doing now?" I asked as I scooted a little closer to her on the bench.

She blinked up at me. "Trying not to kiss you," she said flatly.

Her answer startled me, and I laughed again. "How's that working out?" I asked when I brought my gaze level with hers again.

"Not very well. I'm succeeding, but it's taking more effort than I'd like to admit."

Reaching for her, I tugged her into my lap. "No fair," she teased as she turned to me, her lips inches from mine.

I meant to say something else, something witty, but I found all

I could do was kiss her. It was the logical choice after all, and definitely the most fun.

The moment I fit my mouth over hers, Belle shifted closer to me, one hand cupping my cheek as her other arm wound around my shoulders. She was warm and soft, a contrast to the cool air outside.

I had no idea how long that kiss lasted, because I was gone the second her tongue darted out in a sensual tease against mine. I could kiss Belle forever. That was one of the things I'd never forgotten about her. It wasn't about getting to whatever might come next. Every moment along the way was decadently good.

A horn honked in the parking lot by Speakeasy, the sound carrying through the trees to us. We abruptly broke apart, and I gulped in several lungfuls of crisp autumn air, needing the coolness to clear my head.

"Come home with me, sweetheart," I murmured as I trailed my thumb along the edge of her jaw.

She looked at me quietly for a moment, and I thought she might turn me down. But she didn't. She dipped her head and pressed a kiss right at the base of my throat, the subtle touch like a brand on my skin. I had to grit my teeth to keep from kissing her all over and losing myself again.

"Come on."

She shimmied off my lap, and we stood. I didn't even think about it when I reached for her hand. I savored the fact that she didn't pull away and laced her fingers through mine.

A few moments later, we were in my truck, and Belle announced that she wanted to drive with the windows cracked open.

"It might get chilly," I commented as I glanced toward her before I turned onto the road.

"I don't care. Fall air is my favorite."

I was smiling at her, and then she circled her hand in the air. "Are we going anywhere?"

Jesus. That's how ridiculous I was getting over Belle now. I lost track of just about everything but her.

"Yes, ma'am."

She pressed the button to roll her window down slightly as I did the same. Cool air swirled into my truck as I drove toward home. Fall in Vermont meant crisp nights and earthy scents as the leaves fell, slowly carpeting the ground. Occasionally, the scent of wood smoke carried through the air. Because a fire on a chilly autumn evening was what the season called for.

My body was humming with anticipation. We were quiet on the drive. That was another thing I liked about Belle. She didn't seem to feel the need to fill space with chatter. When I turned onto the drive that led to my partially renovated barn, it felt as if my cells tightened with anticipation.

A few minutes later, our footsteps crunched on the gravel as we walked to the door. When we stepped inside, Belle asked, "How come you renovated the upstairs first?"

We stood just inside the doorway in the circle of light cast from the single light bulb mounted in the small entryway right beside the stairs. I looked down to find her wide brown eyes waiting expectantly for my answer. I had to give myself a mental shake to focus.

"The previous owners had already started to renovate upstairs. It was that simple."

"How much have you done downstairs?"

I reached for her hand. Because I needed to touch her.

"I'll show you." I opened the door that led from the entryway into the barn downstairs.

At the moment, it was cast in darkness, although moonlight fell through the windows, bathing it in a silvery glow. The space was wide open. I had torn down the walls left behind from the old horse stalls.

Belle stopped for a minute, and I could practically hear the smile in her voice. "You can do whatever you want with the space." She dropped my hand and spun in a circle with her arms out.

Aside from taking the walls down and reinforcing the supporting beams, the only thing I'd done was to install windows on one side of the barn. What had once been latched half-doors for the animals to look out were now windows that ran the length of the barn and offered a stunning view out over the Green Mountains with rolling hills and orchards.

Tonight, the landscape was bathed in moonlight. Belle's boots echoed on the dusty wooden floor as she crossed over, resting her hands on a wide windowsill.

As if she had a thread attached to me, I followed her over, stopping beside her.

"It's so beautiful," she whispered.

"It is."

I felt her eyes on me and glanced down. Although there wasn't a single light on, it was easy to see her face in the moonlight. Her dark eyes blinked as she searched my face.

I wasn't thinking, but then it seemed whenever I was close to Belle, thought made itself scarce. Angling to face her, I dipped my head, pressing a hot, open kiss on the underside of her jaw. When she made a little sound at the back of her throat and arched toward me, I dropped another kiss, just under her ear, savoring the sound of her raspy sigh followed by a soft whimper.

Then, it felt as if time sped up and slowed down at once. We were kissing, and each kiss melted into the next, a tangle of lips, teeth, and tongues, ragged breaths in between kisses, and the feel of Belle pressed against me, her lush curves a temptation I couldn't resist.

Belle's hands slipped under my T-shirt, cool against my skin. I tugged at her blouse, letting out a growl of satisfaction when I got the buttons undone and discovered she was wearing another lacy bra.

I teased her nipples through the lace, and she dragged her palm over my cock, where it was swollen and pressing against my zipper. Restless and impatient, I flicked the clasp between her breasts and dipped my head to catch one of her nipples with my mouth, grazing my teeth over it as I swirled my tongue.

She gasped my name, her fingers spearing in my hair briefly before she pushed on my shoulder. Before I could ask what she was doing, she unbuttoned my fly with nimble fingers. I hadn't forgotten how bossy she could be, but I was reminded concretely when she slipped a hand in my boxers as she pushed my jeans down, just enough for my cock to bounce free.

Somehow, this encounter had spiraled out of my control. All I could do was let out a ragged groan when she leaned down and I felt her mouth close over the crown of my cock. I laced my fingers in her hair as she sucked me in deeply.

"Fuck, Belle," I muttered when I felt her tongue drag along the underside before she sucked me in again.

I gave her a little tug because I didn't want this to finish now. I wanted to come inside of her. She didn't let me take control, not just yet. She tortured me a little more with several deep sucks and her tongue teasing around the tip of my cock before she straightened.

Her eyes met mine in the moonlight, and she gave me a saucy grin. That was like the sharp lash of a whip, cracking through the air and sending electricity sizzling all the way down my spine and straight to my balls. "Your turn," I murmured as I lifted her against me.

"Where—?" Whatever question she started ended with a gasp when I adjusted her on my hips just enough for her legs to curl around me.

Belle was a lush bundle of curves in my arms. I didn't have far to go. I had a worktable to the side, and I made it over there, sliding her hips on it.

"Now, where was I?" I trailed my fingers in a teasing circle around one nipple and then the other.

She gasped before replying, "I don't know."

"I think..." I dabbled with my lips along the underside of her breast. "Mmm, right here." I swirled my tongue around a taut nipple and played with her breasts just enough until she was crying out. Once again, she was wearing a skirt.

"God, I fucking love your skirts." I pushed the fabric up.

She shimmied, giving me an assist, until her skirt was rumpled around her hips. When I looked at her, with her lips kiss-bitten, the silvery moonlight gilding her, and her knees open for me, my heart kicked against my ribs and need thrummed through me.

I meant to tease, to take it slow, to make her crazy. The problem was, Belle made me absolutely crazy. The minute my fingers found her slippery cleft, I couldn't wait. I needed to be buried inside her.

BELLE

Ty had this crazy effect on me, where I almost lost myself. Everything was pleasure and sensation storming through me, and all I wanted was more. With his fingers teasing me until I was teetering along the edge of a climax, I cried out, feeling bereft when he drew his fingers away.

"Ty," I protested. "I need—"

"I know what you need, sweetheart."

Jesus. When he talked like that, all bossy and clear that he knew just what I needed, I trembled all over.

I heard something thump, followed by the distinct wrinkle of a condom wrapper. In a second, he smoothed it on, protecting us, before he tugged my hips closer to the edge of the table, murmuring, "I seem to like fucking you on tables."

"Ty," I pleaded when I felt the nudge of his thick crown at my entrance.

I was dripping wet, all for him. "Tell me what you need," he murmured

"You. Now," I gasped, because I was beyond shame with him.

"You've got me."

And then, I felt the delicious slide of him filling me. The

stretch was intoxicating, and my head fell to his shoulder as my climax began to threaten.

He fucked me slow and deep, each surge filling me more completely than the last. It was intense and more intimate than anything I'd ever experienced. Everything pulled tight like a string inside. It unraveled slowly, my release rippling in thick waves of pleasure when he was buried deep. I distantly heard myself crying his name and savoring the sound of mine when he shuddered roughly against me.

The last thing I remembered was him carrying me upstairs. We stumbled out of our clothes and into bed. I fell asleep with him holding me close, feeling warm and safe and secure.

Belle's hair was damp as she smiled over at me. She was fresh-faced and pink-cheeked after a shower.

"What time do you need to be in to work today?" I asked.

"Earlier than usual. I'm doing some planning for specials with Phoebe. I should've thought about that last night and had you bring me to get my car."

I shook my head. "It's no problem. I'll drive you to town in just a few minutes if that's all right."

Belle opened her mouth to reply when there was a sharp knock on the door. Her eyes widened curiously, while my gut tightened. I didn't get many visitors, especially not unannounced ones. In fact, I could think of only one person who would show up unannounced like this.

I debated ignoring it, but there was generally no ignoring my father, not when he was in a mulish mood.

I looked at her. "It's probably my father. I'll warn you now, he's likely to be an asshole."

She nodded. "Can I help you deal with him?" she whispered.

I shrugged. "I'm going to tell him I don't have time, which is true. I'm guessing he's on his way up to see my sister in Burlington. Not that they have a great relationship either."

I opened the door right when another knock landed against it. My father stood there. I took the moment to absorb him. Those who knew us as a family often commented that I looked like him. That annoyed the hell out of me.

His once dark hair was liberally salted with silvery gray. He didn't even try to smile. "Good morning," he opened with.

"Hi, Dad."

"I'm on the way to check in with your sister and thought I'd stop to see how this ridiculous project of yours is coming along."

Fuck my life, and fuck my father. He rarely traveled, but I presumed he was doing some kind of weekend getaway with his girlfriend.

My presumption moved beyond speculation when he added, "Cheryl's waiting in the car. We're staying at a bed and breakfast in Burlington."

I debated telling him to fuck off and leave, but I didn't. He pushed past me, his eyes narrowing the moment they landed on Belle.

"This is Belle," I said, gesturing to her.

My father strode quickly to her, holding his hand out.

"Nice to meet you," Belle said politely.

"Tyler Connor, senior," he offered.

Belle merely smiled and dipped her head in acknowledgment after she shook his hand.

"Girlfriend, I suppose," my father said, turning to look back toward me.

I nodded. I didn't really want to chat with my father about any relationship, much less what I had with Belle. Perhaps we hadn't defined it yet, but trying to clarify it with him would only lead to questions. "We actually need to leave," I added.

My father glanced around, his eyes landing back on mine. "Well, it does look good. I still think you're wasting time in this town."

I fought the anger rising inside of me. "Dad, I'm not working for you."

My impatience with my reaction to him was clenching like an icy fist around my heart. I strode past him and out the door. I wasn't going to stand for him trying to insert himself in my morning.

Moments later, I was outside, and I couldn't even enjoy the crisp autumn morning. My father stopped beside me. "Is it serious?"

"What?"

"Your girlfriend," he muttered, gesturing over his shoulder with his thumb.

"It's none of your business."

Blessedly, my father left. I watched his car disappear down my drive, frustrated with myself and the helpless anger I felt in his presence. Turning, I saw Belle coming through the door. She was looping her purse over her shoulder.

I was embarrassed and annoyed as hell she had to see what kind of man my father was. She stopped beside me and blinked up at me. "Well, that was annoying."

I couldn't help the smile that tugged at the corners of my mouth at that. "Annoying?" I prompted.

"Yes. As you warned me, your father's not very nice. I find it annoying he ruined a perfectly nice morning."

Without thinking, I stepped closer and looped my arms around her waist. "Kind of like a fly?"

Belle's lips twisted to the side as she pondered this. "Sort of, but flies are easy to deal with. You just have to swat them. Come to think of it, I suppose it could've been effective to chase him out with a flyswatter."

I threw my head back with a laugh. When I looked back down at her, my heart thumped hard, and I felt a sense of lightness stealing through me, like an unexpected warm breeze. Belle was turning out to be more than I bargained for. My memories of our nights before had sharpened, and our recent nights had more than lived up to my recollection.

But it was more than that. I liked her. A lot. I didn't even know what to make of the sense of protectiveness she expressed about me and my father. I loved how easily she dismissed him as nothing more than a nuisance.

I drove her back to her place and headed back home to do some work downstairs. Working with my hands always helped clear my mind.

On the drive back, my phone rang. I saw my sister's name flash on my dashboard screen and tapped to answer. Before I could get a word out, Jess said, "I think I'm late with my warning."

"You mean that Dad and Cheryl were coming up for a weekend at a bed and breakfast?"

Jess let out a frustrated groan. "Yes. Mom hasn't said a word, but when I called his office, his receptionist told me."

All these years, and our father still didn't know his receptionist thought he was an asshole. About the only thing my father did right was pay people who stayed at his company well. I had to credit him for that, even if I didn't want to. As it was, Elaine still worked there, and for years had been our go-to point of contact if we needed a status update on our father.

"Yeah, well, he stopped by this morning."

"Oh, God, was it awful?"

"Belle was here, so she got to meet him. Fortunately, I gave her a warning. He didn't stay long, and I walked him out."

"Ugh. He texted me and said he wanted to get together for lunch. Why does he do stuff like this? I've even told him I think he's a dick," Jess said, her tone exasperated.

I chuckled, watching as some brightly colored orange leaves scudded across the road in front of me.

"You've been telling me I just need to tell him to fuck off and he'll stop being a jerk to me," I teased.

I could practically see my sister's face, her nose wrinkling and her eyes narrowing. "Change of subject. How are things going with Belle?"

"Well, she spent the night."

"So what?" Jess scoffed. "You are the king of the hookup. Do you actually like her?"

I pondered my sister's question and decided to be honest. "I do, but I'm not sure what she wants. Or what I want, for that matter."

"Don't let our parents' shitty marriage ruin romance for you."

"I could say the same to you," I countered.

I could practically see her eyes rolling, hard. "Whatever. I'm younger than you. You took that job at Speakeasy because you love the town and said it was the kind of life you wanted. A place where people weren't all plastic and fake. You should try to find someone, and Belle sounds great. It's a hot second chance romance."

Now, I was rolling my eyes. "Okay, enough with that. I like Belle and let's just leave it at that for now. Why don't you update me on your love life?"

"Dude, my love life is like a desert. I like it that way."

"Jess," I began.

"Don't start with me. I know I probably shouldn't give you grief either. I'm sorry I couldn't give you a warning on Dad coming by. At least you don't have to have lunch with him."

"You don't *have* to have lunch with him."

"I know I don't," she muttered. "He caught me off guard is all."

"Same here. All right, sis, I gotta go." I turned down my driveway, my truck bouncing a little on the dirt road.

We hung up, and I threw myself into finishing the windowsills downstairs and considering how I wanted to plan the walls. I'd thought I had it all decided and would rent this space out as a separate apartment. And yet, here I was, wondering how to do it in such a way that if I later wanted more space for myself, it would be an easy modification.

Every time Belle sashayed through my thoughts, I shied away.

I wasn't quite comfortable acknowledging, even in the privacy of my own fucking mind, that she was the one who had me wondering if my cynicism around relationships could be overcome.

BELLE

"Heavenly, right?" Audrey prompted, resting her elbows on the counter at the Busy Bean.

"Yes," I said once I finished chewing.

Their baker, a strapping young man named Roderick, had just brought out a fresh batch of bagels, and I'd immediately ordered one. They were, in fact, heavenly.

She cast me a warm smile as she straightened. Just then, Zara came through the door, the bell above the door jingling to announce her arrival.

Audrey turned her smile on Zara, asking, "Are you hungry?"

"Starving." Zara rested her hips on the counter, her shoulders sagging.

"Are you okay?" I asked.

"I'm fine. Our youngest had a fussy night is all. I think I got maybe two hours total between waking up and trying to go back to sleep."

Audrey patted her on the shoulder. "You need a coffee." She turned to the barista who smiled. "Already getting it ready."

"And here, have one of these. They're still hot from the oven and they're delicious," Audrey added, lifting a bagel. "Come to think of it, you should sit down. You're here early."

Zara shuffled over to a table, catching my eye. "Sit with me."

I wasn't going to say no to that. I'd been coming here almost every other day. I loved the little café, plus the coffee was sublime and the baked goods were always yummy. The other plus? I was getting to know Audrey and Zara, and I thought maybe I could be friends with them. I felt silly thinking of it like that, but I'd felt set adrift when it came to the friend situation. Being a total book nerd wasn't always the best for forming friendships. Then, I'd blown my life up and was totally embarrassed about it. My closest friend had moved away after law school. She knew everything that was going on for me, but it's not like we could see each other that often.

It felt like everything in life was some kind of test for me. I couldn't do friendship on my merits. Even thinking about it like that felt silly. The scaffolding that had held me up had fallen away when I dropped out of law school. Making friends felt so tentative, and yet I craved it. I wanted more than friendships based on shared academic achievements.

I sat down across from Zara, and she took a long swallow of her coffee. "I needed that," she said when she set it down.

Audrey crossed over, setting a plate down with a fresh bagel in front of Zara. "Taste it," she ordered.

Zara obediently took a bite. "Ooh, that's good," she said as she finished chewing.

Audrey's eyes twinkled. "So good."

Audrey ended up grabbing a chair and sitting down with us. They chatted about work things for a few minutes before Audrey looked at me with what I promptly learned was a deceptively innocent smile. "So, I saw you leaving with Ty the other night."

I almost choked on my sip of coffee. Zara cast me a rueful smile. "If you haven't figured it out yet, this is a small town. It's very hard to keep secrets around here."

"You kept a secret," Audrey said, lightly tapping her on the shoulder.

I was grateful for the diversion. "Do tell."

Zara rolled her eyes. "When I was pregnant with Nicole, my oldest, I refused to tell anyone who the father was."

"Um, isn't Dave the father?" I asked, almost incredulous.

Having met Dave, I knew Zara's daughter Nicole had the exact same shade of coppery red hair as Dave, which wasn't all that common.

Audrey bit her lip to keep from laughing. Zara narrowed her eyes, shaking her head slightly before turning her attention back to me. "Yes, he is. I thought he was just a summer fling. I didn't even know his last name, and then I turned out to be pregnant."

"Oh. Wow. You didn't know he was a pro hockey player?" I pressed.

Audrey laughed aloud this time. "She was getting it on with a hot hockey star, and she didn't even know it."

Zara took another bite of her bagel, shrugging lightly. After she finished chewing, she added, "Dave came back for another summer vacation with some of his teammates. After that, I told everyone he was the father. To be fair, I did tell my twin brother, Benito. I wanted his help finding him since Benito's a cop. I didn't even have Dave's last name right though, so it was hit or miss."

"That's an impressive secret to keep."

Zara cast me a wry smile. "Rumors would've flown if Nicole didn't have Dave's hair. There are way more guys with dark hair like mine," she said, pointing to her own hair. "Enough of that. My point is, it's hard to keep secrets around here."

"Just ask May," Audrey chimed in.

"What secret is May keeping?" I asked, honestly wondering.

"Oh, she tried to keep her little fling with Alec a secret, but she conveniently forgot that this café opens early, and we share parking. I kept seeing her car at The Gin Mill when they were sneaking around," Audrey said with a grin.

"Aren't they really together?" I pressed.

"Oh, totally. They're in love," Audrey offered.

"What *is* the deal with you and Ty?" Zara asked, effectively ending the foray away from me in this conversation.

"We knew each other in college. Just a hookup." I tried to sound nonchalant, but I wasn't really feeling it.

"I know all about "just a hookup"," Audrey commented with air quotes included.

When I looked her way, she added, "That's what Griffin was. Now we're married, and we have a kid. My whole life is here. I thought I was going to be a chef running a trendy restaurant in Boston, but I'm here with him, and it's the best decision I ever made."

"It's really cool you got to do real chef training," I replied, experiencing a twinge of insecurity. "I love cooking, but for me, it's all been learning on the fly."

Audrey nudged me gently with her elbow, her eyes warm when I glanced up. "Phoebe told me you're doing a great job, but that's boring. Tell us more about you and Ty."

I stared at her, a subtle sense of panic spinning inside me. Audrey couldn't know it, but I was having feelings about my feelings about Ty.

Zara caught my eyes. "Don't stress. No one expects you to keep the world up to speed on your love life." She paused, her eyes sliding to the side. "Actually, some people probably do."

Audrey shrugged.

"Should I stress about the fact people are noticing that there might be a thing with me and Ty? He's the general manager there, even if I don't answer directly to him."

"I mean, maybe it's a problem for you," Zara offered. "But I don't think you're going to get fired over something like that."

"Just don't let it interfere with work," Audrey offered.

At that moment, the door to the café opened and Ty came walking through with Dave. They appeared to be deep in conversation. Zara lifted a hand in a quick wave. Dave's head whipped in her direction. He didn't even hesitate, practically stopping midsentence with Ty and crossing to her. Ty grinned and followed him over.

"Hey," Dave said as he bent low and dropped a kiss on Zara's cheek. He greeted Audrey and then me.

I managed to say something polite, but I was utterly distracted. When Ty's eyes met mine, heat bloomed through me and butterflies spun in my belly. I hoped my cheeks weren't too flushed and looked down at my coffee before taking a sip.

The thing was, I liked Ty. *A lot*. Liking him, especially as much as I did, might be complicated in the small worlds of Colebury and Speakeasy.

21

—

TY

—

The next few weeks flew by. With leaf peepers passing through the small towns in Vermont in droves and Speakeasy's reputation as a fabulous gastropub and beer aficionados' destination, work was hopping. Belle and I settled into a rhythm.

For me, Belle was like a personal gravitational force. I could only take so many days away from her before I was pulled to her again. We'd see each other, and it would be hot, hot, smokin' *hot*. We moved past the rushed sex and took time to savor each other. It felt like we were actually getting to know each other, both intimately speaking and in spending time with each other.

One morning after she'd spent the night, when neither one of us was working that day, I looked over and surprised myself. "Want to go to Burlington with me for the day?"

Belle's eyes whipped to mine, widening slightly. She hesitated, and I added, "I have to pick up some equipment for the brewery at Speakeasy."

That was entirely true. But really, I just wanted to spend the day with Belle. For some reason, I wanted to sound nonchalant, like it was no big deal.

I didn't realize I was holding my breath until she replied, "Okay. I can always do a few errands."

I released my breath slowly, my shoulders relaxing. "My sister will want to grab lunch. Is that cool?"

Apparently, now I was going to introduce her to my sister. That meant something. Something I wasn't ready to ponder all that long.

Once we were in my truck, driving toward Burlington, I asked, "Now that you've been here a little while, what do you think of Speakeasy? Planning to stick around?"

"I love it," she said earnestly. "It's a great restaurant, and it's fun to work there."

"Do you think being a chef is what you want?"

This question had been percolating in my thoughts ever since Belle shared with me why she dropped out of law school. I was admittedly curious about how she was adjusting. She was still the girl I'd once known—always in a hurry when I saw her at work, and she had that little buzz of quirky. Yet, she was a bit more subdued. When groups of staff from work hung out in the bar in the late hours, the girl I knew in college would've been the center of attention. Perhaps starting up a karaoke song, or organizing a silly game. No matter what, she would've been the brightest light in the room. These days, she didn't abstain from drinking, but she didn't drink much, and she tended to hover on the edges of any group.

I felt her shrug. "I think so. Because I love it."

"Do you ever think about law school and your old plans?"

I knew a little bit about plans falling through because mine had. I sensed Belle's experience was pretty different from mine though.

She was quiet for a few beats, and I stole a quick glance at her as I slowed to turn onto the main highway that led to Burlington. She was fiddling with a bracelet on her wrist, a narrow silver cuff. She was tracing her fingertip back and forth over it, as if she were polishing it. Her knee was jiggling, and she glanced sideways, catching me looking at her.

Uncertainty flickered in her eyes, and her cheeks flushed

slightly. "Of course I do," she said softly as I looked ahead again, not because I was avoiding her gaze, but because I did actually need to look at the road in front of me.

"Sometimes I wonder about it, but I can't imagine going back," she added.

"Because you don't want to?"

When I slid my gaze sideways again, she was nodding. "I don't. Well, I don't think I do. I'm much happier than I ever was in law school. But old habits die hard and all that. School was something I was good at, and it came easily. I'm not saying that to brag or anything," she added hurriedly.

"I didn't think you were," I said carefully. "Even when I knew you back in college, of course I knew school was important to you, but you weren't arrogant about it, not at all. And, you were always helping anyone who asked. If I recall, you even offered to help me with a math class that I complained about."

Belle's throaty laugh filled the truck cab, and my body jolted with a sizzle of electricity in response. I wasn't thinking about sex, but I couldn't help my reaction to her. It just happened, as easily as goosebumps on my skin when I was too cold.

"I always did like to be helpful. Still do. You know," she said, almost as if she were talking to herself. "Maybe I should do tutoring at the high school."

"I'm sure they'd be glad to have you. Do you want to do that? That sounds miserable to me. Tutoring doesn't exactly sound fun."

"Don't you coach for the local hockey league for kids?" she countered, smiling when I glanced over.

"I do. Because hockey is definitely *my* thing."

A laugh rustled in her throat. "Back to your original question, yes, I love it at Speakeasy. Phoebe's great to work for, and I've learned a lot from her. I like it here in town."

"What exactly happened when you dropped out?"

Although Belle had given me the broad strokes, I was still trying to wrap my brain around what prompted her to drop out.

Her deep breath was audible. "Like I told you, the pressure was getting to me. I was super anxious and constantly tense. My doctor and my therapist both tell me I was on my way to a manic episode no matter what, but it definitely pushed me over the edge to be putting that much pressure on myself. Things just got out of control, and then I ended up in the hospital. It was only one night. It really threw me into a tailspin afterwards. I had some trouble with the school because of what happened, so I dropped out. I needed the time to get myself together. I stayed with my parents for a while, and a friend who worked at a restaurant in Burlington knew a place that needed someone to fill-in in the kitchen while the main chef was on maternity leave. She knew I was a good cook, so I slipped right in. It turned out to be great. I already knew I loved to cook, but I really hit my stride there. It suits my personality. Honestly, even though I'm on medication, that need to be on the move is there no matter what. I guess it's part of my personality. When I'm cooking, I can be creative and have fun and it just works. Don't get me wrong, there *is* pressure, but it's not the kind of pressure that makes me anxious the way academic stuff did. It's weird."

"I get it. I don't want to work for my dad because I can't tolerate that type of pressure. I mean, he's also an asshole, but I have zero interest in dealing with the pressure of managing investments and all that. But the pressure of hockey," I shrugged. "It really didn't get to me."

"How has that change been for you?"

Her question fell softly in the space between us.

I thought for a moment. "Honestly, it's okay. I was always pretty realistic about the odds. Don't get me wrong, I hate that it was an injury that threw me off because it wasn't on my merits. But maybe that would've been harder to deal with anyway, if you know what I mean."

"I get that. I'm sorry for you. You were so good."

"It was fun while it lasted."

She was quiet for a moment before adding, "It would've been

nice if I could've figured out what I wanted before blowing my life up."

"It doesn't sound like you blew your life up."

She snorted.

"I think you're being too hard on yourself, by the way."

"Why do you say that?"

"You're obviously doing okay. Maybe things didn't go so well for a little bit there, but it wasn't like you hurt anyone. As far as I can tell, you've got your shit together and you're doing something you love."

Belle's laugh was a little bitter. "You have no idea. But thank you. I *am* doing okay now, and I intend to keep it that way. I figured out a medication that works for me, and I know how to keep an eye on myself so I don't let things spiral out of control again."

I caught her gaze again. "It sounds like you know what you need. That's pretty important to figure out."

22

BELLE

Because my habits of being a dutiful daughter were deeply ingrained in me and because I loved my parents, I sent them a quick text that I was doing errands and having lunch in Burlington. I didn't want them to think I was going out of my way *not* to see them. If they wanted me to pop by, I would ask Ty to take a quick detour.

My mother texted that she was tied up in classes all day, and my father had client meetings.

We were hoping to come have dinner at Speakeasy again soon, my mother said with a smiley emoticon.

I glanced to Ty as he pulled into a space in a parking lot. "Well, you won't have to meet my parents. They're both busy."

He grinned. "Is that good or bad?"

"Neutral. I love my parents, but I didn't want you to feel weird if they wanted to see me."

"I already met them, Belle." When I looked askance at him, he added, "When they came to Speakeasy."

"Oh, right."

"Plus, I'm introducing you to my sister. Is that weird?"

We stared at each other across the seat in his truck. I felt my cheeks flushing as my lips curled into a smile. "I don't know," I finally said. "Is it weird?"

The moment suddenly felt serious.

"I don't think so," Ty said. "I think you'll like Jess."

The moment passed, and we went about our day. Ty picked up the supplies for Speakeasy, and we met his sister at a sandwich shop.

Jess shared Ty's coloring, except her dark hair was long. Somehow, Ty had thicker eyelashes, which seemed inherently unfair since he was a man. We had a friendly lunch, and she walked outside the café with us. She just barely had a limp.

When we were standing outside, she glanced from me to Ty and back again, a sly glint in her eyes. "You make sure he treats you right," she teased.

Ty narrowed his eyes. "Really, Jess?"

I laughed. Being an only child, I'd always slightly envied the teasing relationships between siblings. "He does treat me well. Should I call you if he doesn't?"

Ty's eyes shifted to me, widening slightly. "Don't you dare."

Jess cast me a warm smile, stepping close and pulling me into a quick hug. It was only then I noticed one of her arms didn't lift completely.

"It was awesome to meet you. I promise, he's the best kind of guy, even if he hides it well sometimes."

She hugged Ty after that, and we waved as we climbed into his truck. A few minutes after we were back on the highway, Ty offered, "I hope Jess didn't make you uncomfortable."

"Not at all. It's nice you two are actually close. Not all siblings are."

"Definitely not. I feel blessed. Do you have any?"

"Nope. Just me. Every so often when I was little, I wished I had a brother or a sister, but my parents are great, so I have no complaints on the family front."

"That's a good thing. Jess and I are close, in part because we bonded over our shitty father."

"What about your mother?"

He shrugged. "I have a decent relationship with her. She was crazy overprotective of Jess. You probably noticed Jess has a limp. That's from the car accident. Burns are scary."

"How old were you when that happened?" I was trying really hard not to think about what I hadn't told Ty. I wasn't ready for him to know about my brush with the law, but I had to swat my shame away.

"Eight." Ty looked ahead steadily, but I noticed the tightening around his eyes and at the corners of his mouth.

"I imagine that was hard for you."

He gave a one-shouldered shrug. "It was definitely much harder for Jess."

Ty deftly changed the subject, and I realized perhaps his family was a sore spot for him. No judgment from me on that score.

A little while later when Ty took the exit off the highway toward Colebury, he asked, "Want me to drop you off?"

My heart gave a funny little tumble, and anxiety tightened in my chest. Because I didn't want him to drop me off. I wanted to stay with him. This day, although it was filled with mundane activities, errands and getting lunch, felt somehow momentous.

"You can if you want," I said, trying to keep my tone nonchalant. "You don't have to though."

"Then, I won't."

That was the very first time I spent two nights in a row with him. Two nights turned into three and then four. Every single night, I could forget everything except how good it felt to be in thrall to Ty. The man knew how to make me fly. He handled me with a deft mix of bossy and tender, taking turns being commanding and filthy, and gentle and sensual.

I knew I was falling for him, and the anxiety I'd been trying to hold at bay was spinning faster and tighter inside whenever I let myself think about it.

23

TY

Belle's brown eyes blinked as she peered up at me. All she was doing was standing by the door and shrugging into her jacket. My heart flipped in my chest and a fierce emotion coursed through me. Stepping closer, I slipped an arm around her waist before dipping my head to kiss her. I almost couldn't tolerate the intensity of my feelings, so I poured them into a devouring kiss.

She made a surprised sound in her throat and flexed into me. Touching her eased the storm of emotion inside, and I managed to gentle our kiss before lifting my head. "See you later," I murmured.

She blinked again, surprise flickering in her eyes. Maybe I didn't speak aloud about how unsettled I felt, but I could tell she sensed it. The moment spun out before she nodded and stepped back. I missed the feel of her curves imprinted against me instantly.

"You will." Just when I thought she'd turn and leave, she leaned up and kissed me quickly, her lips brushing across mine like the lick of a flame.

Then, she was gone in a whirl, and I listened to the sound of her boots striking the stair treads as she hurried downstairs. I walked slowly across the room, stopping in front of the windows.

I rested my palms flat on the windowsill and stared out over the view. The Green Mountains had a dusting of snow on a few taller peaks. Melting hoarfrost glittered where the sun's rays angled across the landscape.

I was falling in love with Belle, and I didn't know what the hell to do about it. On the list of things I hadn't planned for in life, falling in love was near the top. Fuck. I had no freaking clue how to do love. My parents' disaster of a marriage was no help whatsoever. I'd honestly, and apparently naively, thought I'd never have to worry about it. I'd assumed I could just decide I wouldn't fall in love. So much for that.

A few days later

"What the hell are you talking about, Dad?" I said into my phone. I held it against my ear with one hand as I dusted the sawdust off a worktable downstairs in the barn with my other hand.

He hadn't called since that morning when he showed up unexpectedly and saw Belle here. For which I'd been grateful. He usually only called to nag me anyway.

"Your little girlfriend isn't being upfront with you," he said.

"Dad, I really don't want to discuss anyone in my personal life with you and please don't refer to Belle like that."

"Did she tell you she got arrested for car theft?"

I couldn't help the shocked question that slipped out. "What?"

"I didn't think you knew. Yep. I did some digging. You'd best know who you're getting involved with."

"Oh, my God, Dad. I don't think Belle—"

"I thought you should know she got arrested for car theft, and then the charges were dropped. Looks like some kind of inside favor. Probably because of her family. Since both of her parents are attorneys, I'm sure they know their way around the legal system."

Even though my thoughts were skidding into a tailspin over this, I didn't want to hear more from my father, most definitely not speculation. "Dad, I've gotta go."

I ended the call abruptly. I was pissed at my dad, but I was also confused. Him digging into someone in my life wasn't a surprise. He was both distant and intrusive. He was a sledgehammer of a personality, just driving right at things and not caring what or who he harmed in the process.

Belle was arrested for stealing a car? I was going to have to ask her about it. I didn't like how that felt. It wasn't as if she owed me her entire life story. And yet, this hit uncomfortably close to home for me, considering what happened to my sister.

I couldn't even wrap my brain around the how and why Belle would somehow have stolen a car. It made no sense. Much as I loathed my father, I didn't doubt his information was accurate. Fuck.

I spun away from the table, running a hand through my hair. I put away my tools for the day and jogged upstairs to shower. I needed to get into town because I promised Alec I'd help him move something from his apartment. As I drove into town a while later, I mulled over how to talk to Belle. I wondered what else she hadn't told me, and more importantly, why she didn't trust me to tell me. I was feeling edgy.

Belle was starting to matter. *A lot.* I felt too unsettled about whether or not I could trust her.

After several nights in a row together, we'd both been busy, and our schedules had fallen out of alignment. I'd had to cover some late nights at the bar because of one thing or another, and Belle was busy at work as always.

I pulled into the parking lot at The Gin Mill, waving when I saw Alec tossing some trash in the dumpster. Climbing out, I called over, "You still need a hand this afternoon?"

"If you've got a few," he replied.

"That's why I'm here." I stopped beside him, and he gestured over to a truck parked behind The Gin Mill. A mattress covered in plastic was in the back. "We have to carry it all the way up to the third floor."

"Let's do it," I said, crossing over and eyeing the mattress.

A few minutes later, after we grunted our way up two flights of stairs, I leaned against the wall to catch my breath. "No wonder May didn't want to help," I offered with a chuckle.

Alec flashed a grin. "She doesn't know."

"Oh, you're surprising her with a new mattress."

He nodded. "Yep. She's gonna love it."

"So, a mattress is a sign of true love then?" I teased as he opened the door.

We hefted the mattress up again, and he replied, "I don't know. I've only been in love once. I got a deal on this, and I wanted to surprise her with it. She's at work all day, so I figured now's the time."

We went down a hallway and into a room. The entire space was nice with exposed brick walls, glossy hardwood floors, and the like. Situated on the top floor of the old mill building that housed The Gin Mill, their apartment definitely had atmosphere.

We both let out a heavy sigh as we settled the mattress on the bed frame. There was another mattress already propped against the wall. "Need help carrying that one down?" I asked.

"I wasn't going to ask, but it would be nice. I'd usually have my brother Benito help, but he's busy today."

"Hey, we did the hard part and carried this one up. With that one, we have gravity on our side when we go down the stairs," I commented.

"See, I knew it was smart to ask you," he replied with a wink.

We carried the old mattress down, and then I followed Alec back upstairs when he offered some iced tea. After a swallow, I glanced around. "You renovate this whole place yourself?"

"I had some help, but for the most part it was me."

"Between this building, and your investment in Speakeasy, looks like you've really made a difference to this area."

Alec shifted his shoulders. "I guess so. May helped me with all the legal stuff as far as my partnership with Lyle, Griffin, and my uncle. That made a big difference for me. Without her handling all the legal details, I don't know if I could've pulled it off."

I found myself actually wanting to ask Alec for some relationship advice. But holy shit was that uncomfortable. I held his gaze, with my question slipping out before I could think too much about it. "How did you know?"

"How did I know what?"

"That May was the one for you."

He eyed me curiously, but he didn't tease. "Oh, is this about your thing with Belle?"

"Jesus," I muttered. "No such thing as privacy around here, is there?"

Alec's laugh rustled in his throat. "It's a small town, people notice things. Long as it's not interfering with your work, no worries on my part."

I took another swallow of tea. Alec was gracious enough to go back to my question. "I don't know exactly how I knew. What surprised me about May was I was all about just having a good time, no strings, no complications. That's pretty much how it started with me and her. I think it crept up on both of us. It felt right, if that makes any sense."

I nodded slowly. Because it totally made sense. That was the funny thing about Belle. That easy feeling I had with her that all started around sex was expanding to everything. I didn't feel like I had to be anything or anyone other than precisely who I was with her.

Alec gave me a long look before adding, "When it's good and it feels right, I call that really lucky."

I finished my glass of tea and set it on the counter. We were standing in the kitchen. "It's kind of funny that May doesn't drink and you own two bars," I observed.

He shrugged. "I suppose. We make it work. Although I like running a bar and I enjoy getting into all the stuff around brewing, alcohol is not a big part of my life personally. I never even worried about that."

Although I didn't know May too well, she was pretty open that she was in recovery, so I was prompted to ask, "How does she feel about it?"

"It was something we had to talk about, but it's not an issue for us. When someone's important, that's what matters." Alec, who was inclined to tease, gave me an intent look, his gaze solemn, and I couldn't help but wonder if he saw more than I even understood about my own questions.

A short while later when I got to Speakeasy, Belle was zipping around the kitchen as she was wont to do whenever she was working. She looked up as I passed by her, heading into the bar. Our eyes collided for a moment, and it felt as if sparks sizzled in the air between us.

I didn't like that I couldn't put it out of my mind that maybe things had been messier than she'd led me to believe, messy being stealing a car. I didn't like that she was hiding something and wondered what else she might be hiding. I hated that she didn't trust me enough to be honest.

24

—

TY

—

Even though I knew I needed to ask Belle about what my father told me, even though it was the mental equivalent of a blister, I ignored it. I was furious with my father—for nosing into my life, for ripping into Belle's, and for making me question the woman I'd fallen in love with and forcing me to wrestle with just how tricky trust could be. Not ready to face the conversation with Belle and all it represented, I chose to lose myself in our fiery connection.

Belle made me crazy, in all the right ways, so it was easy to get lost in us. She also thoroughly disabused me of the notion that I had some semblance of control. One night after work when I was feeling greedy, we found each other at the bench I was starting to think of as ours.

She was sitting beside me, her mere presence a distraction. I dipped my head and dropped a string of kisses along the side of her neck as I tugged her closer. She tasted sweet, and her scent curled around me. My teeth grazed her earlobe, and she shivered.

Next thing I knew, her hand was stealing under the hem of my shirt. She slid her palm around my waist and murmured into my chest, "It's not fair."

"What's not fair?" My lips moved against her skin where I was teasing over her collarbone.

"You're in such good shape."

"I still play hockey, just for fun now."

Belle lifted her head. "Plus, you do all that hard labor working on your barn."

My lips tugged into a grin. "Sure. That also helps."

Impatient for more, I nipped at her neck and found my way back to her mouth. I palmed her cheek, angling her head to the side as I took her mouth with a deep, devouring kiss. I didn't want to stop, but I forced myself to draw back.

"You don't get to stop that soon," she murmured.

She shifted and climbed onto my lap, straddling me. She took the lead, cupping my cheeks, diving into my mouth again, and letting out a little moan when I reflexively rocked my arousal against her.

Within minutes, I had one hand under her shirt, copping a liberal feel of her breasts, while she leaned back and let out a gasp when my fingers pinched her nipple through the silk of her bra.

"Belle." My voice was gruff.

She rocked her hips restlessly.

"What?" she finally gasped.

"We should go."

"Why?"

"Because we're outside. I'm all about a little risky fun, but people do frequent this path."

Dragging her eyes open, she gulped in a breath. "You're right, let's go to my place. It's closer."

That worked for me. I lifted her off my lap, and a little tremor ran through her.

"I'll drive us even though it's not far. That way, my truck is there in the morning," I commented as I curled my hand around hers and led us through the trees.

Only a few minutes later, our fingers were still laced together as we stumbled up the stairs to her apartment.

As soon as we made it into her apartment, I kicked the door shut behind us, spinning her against it and diving into another breath stealing kiss.

Her tongue dueled with mine, and one of her naughty hands slid between us, stroking boldly over my cock. I let out a ragged groan into her mouth, lifting my head to gulp in some air.

She nipped lightly at my neck, pushing my jacket off my shoulders. That's how it was with her, so often a mad tangle and a rush to get closer.

"Bed," I murmured as I stepped back from the door, lifting her against me.

She was excellent at following instructions and curled her legs around my waist. She pointed across the living room. There was a lamp on in the corner, casting just enough light for me to see this was one of those common modified spaces in old houses. There was a small efficiency kitchen to one side with a table serving as a divider between that and the living room. I could see the lights of the other houses across the green glittering through the window. When I reached one of the doors, she tapped it with her foot.

"Good guess. The other one's the bathroom. Though we could go for a shower if you wanted," she teased, her voice husky.

"Later."

I took her mouth in another heated kiss as I eased her down from my hold. Our clothes came off rapidly, tossed here and there. My body was humming with need, tightening when I glanced down to see her shimmying backward on the bed. She was bare naked, and that was exactly what I needed. I caught her by one ankle.

She stilled, her lashes swinging up as she looked up at me. "What?" Her chin lifted, and there was that saucy, almost daring look in her eyes that spurred the need already driving me.

"This." I dipped my head as I knelt down, dropping a hot kiss on the inside of her ankle, savoring the way she trembled all over. "This." Another kiss on the inside of her knee.

"Ty," she gasped, a little whimper escaping. "Hurry."

"Not this time, sweetheart." That was said in between kisses as I made my way up her legs.

Who was I kidding? Even I couldn't drag things out but so long. The moment I got close to the apex of her thighs, my eyes landed on the core of her. She was slick with arousal. Pressing her knees apart, I gripped her hips with one hand when she bucked into my mouth.

I made love to her with my lips and tongue, bringing her to a climax that had her shuddering on the bed and gasping my name. Only then did I give in to her urging and rise up. I'd had enough forethought to toss a condom on the bed when I was getting out of my jeans.

Our heads butted when she tried to be helpful as I rolled it on. She was giggling when my weight came down over her. "Hang on," I murmured. Holding her close, I spun us over together, shifting back until I was propped up against her pillows.

Belle bit her lip as I lifted my eyes to meet hers. She blinked, and for just a second, I saw vulnerability flickering in the depths of her gaze. She hid it well, but I knew she was feeling adrift these days.

Something about her tonight kicked open another door into my heart. I lifted a hand, brushing her tousled hair away from her eyes. "There. Now, you can ride me."

She liked that, a sensual smile curling her lips. She rocked her hips, her slippery cleft sliding over the underside of my cock. Impossible though it seemed, I swelled even further.

When she rose up slightly, I reached between us and felt the slick kiss of her arousal on the tip of my cock. She held still for a beat before sliding down and sheathing me in her snug, clenching core. My head thumped against the headboard behind me when she settled down firmly and wiggled her hips slightly, as if making sure she had it just right.

The thing was, being like this with Belle was always just right. It didn't matter if we fumbled. It all felt good.

She let out a low hum, and I dragged my eyes open. She

blinked again, and I felt her channel clench when I nudged my hips slightly. We stared at each other for several echoing beats of my heart. Her breath came in soft pants and intimacy curled like smoke around us.

Then, she began to move. I gripped her hips loosely as we rocked together. She was chasing after her release almost instantly, and I was spun so tight for release, so was I.

With each stroke into the very heart of her, I felt the brush of her nipples against my chest. I pressed my thumbs over her clit, catching her cry with a kiss when she rippled around me. It felt like a crack of thunder followed by a sizzle of lightning when my release whipped through me.

Awareness came in fragments. The soft gust of her breath on my shoulder where she had tucked her chin. Her fingertips idly tracing across my collarbone. The echo of my heartbeat gradually slowing.

I wanted to shy away from my thoughts, like a nervous horse. With Belle a warm bundle in my lap, it was impossible for my treacherous heart not to thrash in my chest.

I hadn't meant to let anyone mean too much to me. I'd thought I was immune. She had gone and thoroughly proven me wrong. I knew why I'd gotten so out of sorts by what my father discovered. I didn't like to think she might keep secrets. I didn't like to think why that would matter so much to me.

I had to talk to her soon. I couldn't keep avoiding it.

When I woke the following morning, Belle was warm and soft beside me. As the haze of sleep cleared, it felt as if a cold wind gusted through me. I didn't want to confront her with what I knew, but I couldn't hold it inside anymore. She didn't trust me enough to be honest, and I couldn't keep hiding what I knew if that mattered to me. It fucking hurt that she'd been holding back.

It hurt way more than I wanted to face. When I felt the press of her lips on my shoulder, I closed my eyes again. The fucked up thing was I loved being with her, and that was why this mattered.

I forced myself to sit up, shifting back to rest my shoulders against the headboard. Belle propped herself on an elbow, her eyes swinging up to mine. That cold sensation deepened and dread coiled inside of me, but I forced myself to speak.

"Tell me something, I was wondering if maybe you had legal problems."

25

BELLE

"What?"

"I was wondering if maybe you had legal problems," Ty repeated.

We were still in bed. In *my* bed. Only moments ago, I'd pressed a kiss on his shoulder, thinking it was awfully nice to wake up with him. Now this. Ugh. He was sitting up and leaning against the headboard. His lips were pinched at the corners, and his eyes held a guarded look.

My heart kicked into an unsteady beat, and I felt a little sick. That feeling was followed immediately by a wave of shame and embarrassment. All of those things I was so tired of feeling. I wanted a fresh start, and I had one, but Ty was a complication. And, dammit, I was pretty sure I was falling in love with him.

I took a deep breath, reminding myself I *had* screwed up, but I had done what I could to put things to rights.

I looked over at him and forced the words out. "Yes. Everything I told you before was true, it's just I left out some of the messier and more embarrassing details. When I was manic, I was feeling… I don't know how to describe it, like nothing could be a bad decision, nothing at all, and I…I…" I paused and took a shaky breath.

I was stumbling over my words and that only revved up my anxiety. I scrambled for purchase inside, trying to get my balance mentally and grasping for some courage.

I straightened, leaning over and reaching for a tank top tossed on a chair near my bed. Maybe it was pointless, but I needed to not be completely naked for this conversation. Tugging it on, I sat cross legged and turned toward him.

Ty's eyes were intent on me as we faced each other.

"Being manic is a weird feeling. It feels amazing and stressful at the same time."

He arched a brow, and I forged ahead. "Look, I don't have all the words to make it make sense to someone who hasn't experienced it. But when I was manic, I didn't think clearly about anything. I don't even know why, but I stole one of my professor's cars."

It took an effort to swallow through the tightness in my throat. I forced myself not to be a coward and look away from Ty. "I was already horrified and embarrassed about it, and then I found out about your sister's accident, and I didn't know how to tell you."

I couldn't read his gaze. He gave a barely perceptible nod, and I forged ahead. "I didn't even think I thought of it as stealing, even though it obviously was. The keys were in the little cupholder thing," I offered pointlessly. "I don't know what I was thinking because I had my own car there. I got arrested. Instead of putting me in jail, they ended up taking me to the hospital because I'm pretty sure I said some confusing stuff. I went to stay with my parents after that, and that's when I reconnected with May." He nodded along, as if what I was saying made sense. "May helped me work everything out after connecting me with a friend of hers who works for a pro bono program. The professor was kind enough to drop the charges. I did some community service and found a good therapist and psychiatrist, and there you have it. That's the only crime I've ever committed."

Ty stayed silent, and panic spun in a tight circle in my chest.

"If you think this makes me too messed up to be my friend, or whatever it is that we are, I totally get it."

I didn't like how nervous I felt, but I managed to keep breathing. He regarded me quietly. All the while, I could hear the echoing thump of my heart, drumming out an anxious, staccato beat. His silence stretched just long enough that I felt compelled to say more. "Look, I get it if it's weird. I should've told you that sooner. It's just... Well, it's embarrassing. It's really hard to explain just how monumentally bad my judgment was at the time."

Leaning forward and resting his elbows on his knees, he finally spoke, "Makes sense."

His voice was gruff, and I didn't know what he was thinking. I didn't know what to make of what he said. "It makes sense?"

"Well, yeah. I can't say I've been manic, but after you told me about it, I did look it up. Not you, but the diagnosis. I don't remember everything I read, and I didn't want to dwell. But it seems like people experiencing that can do things that are out of character, therefore your explanation makes sense."

"Oh," I said softly. My hands were curled into the sheets, and I only noticed it because they were clenched so tight.

"So, is this a deal breaker?" I finally asked the question that scared me the most.

"I think I understand why you didn't mention it sooner. Does anyone else know?"

I didn't miss that he didn't answer my question.

I finally lifted my head, even though I was nervous to meet his eyes. Peering up at him, I said, "Just the police who arrested me, the hospital, the social worker who works at the police station, the professor whose car I stole, a few witnesses who saw me take off with it, my parents and any of their friends who heard about it, and May Shipley and the pro bono attorney who helped me clean up the mess I made." After I listed all those people, I realized how ridiculous it was that I ever thought I could keep this detail a secret.

Ty's eyes searched mine.

Because I was never all that good at shutting up, I added, "So, maybe you could see why I might want a fresh start. I didn't come here to run away. All I wanted was a peaceful fresh start. Then, I ran into you." I twisted my lips at that and rolled my eyes.

"I didn't mean to ruin your fresh start," he said, returning my eyeroll. "Plus, I knew you and was really glad to find you again."

My heart felt split open at his words, and I instantly scolded myself. *All he said was he was "really glad" to find me. Don't read too much into it.*

"You knew the me who liked to party and who thought being valedictorian was the best thing in life." I didn't know why I felt the need to point that out, but there I went.

"Do you want that life back though?"

I shook my head quickly.

"If there's one thing I understand, it's learning what matters in life."

"So, it's not a deal breaker?"

Once again, he didn't address my question. "We all have stuff."

"A major mental health diagnosis and a history of car theft may be more than the average stuff," I said wryly.

"That's not the problem."

Okay, so there *was* a problem. Well, I *knew* there was a problem, I just didn't know how major the problem was for Ty.

"How did you find out?" I finally asked.

"My father looked you up and told me." Bitterness chased through his eyes. "He can be an ass. I'm sorry he did that, but I'm not sorry I know." He paused and looked down at his lap, long enough for my anxiety to start churning in my chest again.

When his eyes lifted again, I wasn't sure how to read what I saw there. "I know you're not like the guy who caused my sister's accident, but it hit close to home. After watching my parents' mess of a marriage, trust doesn't come easy for me."

His words came out with quiet deliberateness.

I swallowed through the thick knot in my throat and blinked back the tears threatening. When I chanced a look in his eyes, he was watching me intently. His next words went through me like a cold knife.

"The problem is you didn't trust me to tell me." His shoulders rose and fell with a slow breath. "It wouldn't even matter if I didn't think I loved you."

Pausing again, he leaned his head down, running his hands swiftly through his hair in a frustrated gesture. When he looked up again, my stomach plummeted as if I'd just fallen from a great height. He'd just told me he thought he loved me, and I couldn't even enjoy it.

"I need some time."

I cut in. "Ty—"

He shook his head, his gaze disappointed. Or, at least, that's what I thought. I fancied myself an expert at knowing when I'd disappointed someone.

"If you think this has anything to do with anything other than that you didn't trust me to be honest, it doesn't. I don't care about all the details, but it *really* fucking matters that you didn't trust me." He kicked the sheets off his legs and stood from the bed swiftly. I was frozen in place, my hands curling tighter into the sheets as I watched him yank his clothes on.

When he looked down at me, the tears felt locked in my chest. "I've known for days. I thought I could ignore it. If we were just hooking up, maybe I could. But you mean more than that, enough that it burns to know you don't trust me. Were you ever planning to tell me?"

I shrugged because I hadn't thought that far ahead. "I'm sorry," I whispered through my aching throat.

"I know you are, but I think you need to figure something out before you can really be with someone."

Blinking hard, I stared up at him. "What?"

"You make a big deal about having Bipolar Disorder, and I

think you think it's this huge thing that would turn people off. It's not. It's not at all. I couldn't fucking care less about that, but you have to be honest. That *is* a deal breaker for me."

26

TY

If only I could've persuaded myself that I didn't miss Belle. That was impossible. The job I loved now felt like playing a game of hide and seek. Belle and I seemed caught in an unwilling game of avoidance, while the desire to see her had me stealing small glances of her whenever I could.

A few days after I told Belle I needed a break, I was passing through the kitchen at Speakeasy and my gaze was drawn to her as if she were my own personal lodestone. She was busy doing something, but then she was always on the move at work. My eyes landed on the back of her neck. I wanted to cross the kitchen swiftly and drop my head to kiss her there. I wanted to peel her shirt down and kiss her tattoo. My memory called up the scent of her instantly—musky and often with a hint of sugar. I forced my eyes away and left. My shift was over, and I didn't need to linger.

At home a little while later, I drained a beer and tossed the empty bottle in the recycling bin under the sink. I flung myself on my couch, idly turning on the television and telling myself a little distraction would help. Newsflash: it didn't. Avoiding Belle wasn't helping, and I missed her so much that I ached. It was almost a physical experience with my heart sore, and my gut tight. I gave up and went to bed, tossing and turning and reaching for her in the night.

The following morning when my phone rang, I snatched at it, reflexively looking at the screen and pointlessly hoping to see Belle's name appear there. It didn't, but I was surprised to see my mother calling. We didn't talk too often. I slid my thumb across the screen.

"Hi, Mom."

"Hi, Ty," she replied. "How are you?"

"Fine," I lied. "You?"

"Uh, well, I've adjusted to Jess being gone." She laughed dryly. "I don't call her every day now. You know I worry about her, but I'm glad she got into that graduate program, and I'm grateful you two are near each other."

"She seems to be doing well," I offered. "How are things at home?"

"Well, I've been busy." She paused, and I sensed she wanted to say something. We tended to hew to the superficial in our conversations, so I was curious. "Ty, I'll just get right to it. Perhaps I'm nosing into things, but your father mentioned to me you were seeing someone, and he further mentioned he had looked into her background. I'm sorry he did that."

I gritted my teeth, breathing through the sharp pain in my heart. She continued. "It's nothing I didn't expect. I know he wouldn't have done that if he didn't think you cared about her. I hope you're not letting that get in the way."

I sighed, leaning my head back and staring at the ceiling before lowering my gaze to look out the windows. The landscape was blurred with the rain, which suited my mood.

"Mom, it's not what dad thinks. Belle has Bipolar Disorder. The car thing happened when she was in a manic phase. We're taking a break. Not because of that, but because she didn't tell me."

"Didn't tell you what?" my mother prompted.

"Well, she didn't tell me about getting arrested for stealing a car. Trust is an issue for me. I'm sure you can guess why."

My mother was quiet for several long beats before speaking. "Of course, I understand why. Your father and I don't exactly have a healthy relationship. I know you don't understand why I've stayed, and maybe someday I'll leave. All I can say is it was too much for me to try to tear things apart after your sister's accident. If you love this Belle, give her a chance."

I absorbed my mother's words, not even sure how to respond at first. Clearing my throat, I replied, "I'll try."

"I hope you will. You always were a kind boy. Even if we never talked about it, I knew you never intended to get serious with anyone. It's not worth holding onto resentment over something you had no control over."

I wasn't quite sure what she meant, but I sensed she was referring to my sister's accident. Although my mother spent years worrying over Jess, she'd never shown a hint of resentment.

As if she could read my thoughts, my mother commented, "I used to, but I moved on. I'm sure if your sister hadn't survived, I might feel differently. Clinging to anger never helps anything. Whether it's this girl, or another. Don't be afraid."

While my mother's words rang like a gong in my thoughts, she deftly moved the conversation onto more superficial matters after that. After we ended the call and seconds after I set the phone down, it rang again. This time it was my sister.

Bemused, I answered. "Hey, Jess. It's family morning. Mom just called."

"Ah. She told me."

"What do you mean?" I asked, even though I already knew her answer.

"About Belle."

I sighed, wondering what to tell Jess.

"What's the real story? Because I know Belle's not a criminal, even if she did steal a car." Jess snorted at that, and I could imagine her nose wrinkling.

I quickly summarized, wondering in the back of my mind if I was violating Belle's privacy. But this seemed the better option than having Jess think she stole a car for the fun of it.

"So, that makes sense," Jess said.

"It does?"

"I said it makes sense, so it does," she repeated, her tone carrying a hint of annoyance.

I realized I'd said the very thing to Belle when she explained the series of events.

"How are things with you and Belle?"

Fuck. I didn't need to try to explain myself to Jess, but there was no way to avoid it.

"I told her I needed a break," I finally said.

"Why?"

"Because she lied to me about this. She didn't tell me what happened. I can't deal with that. You, of all people, should understand."

"Did she actually lie?" Jess pressed. "Or, did she just not tell you?"

"There's lying by commission and by omission," I muttered. "She didn't tell me."

"Given how you responded, maybe she was worried about your reaction. You've gone and proved her right on that account," Jess snapped. "How do you feel about her?"

My heart gave an achy thump, and I gritted my teeth. I decided to tell my sister the truth. "I think I love her."

"Well, then, don't be stupid."

"Jess, I'm sure even you can agree it's pretty crazy I'd end up falling for a girl who stole a car. You almost died because of someone who stole a car."

She cut in swiftly. "No, I almost died because the guy was drunk and ran into us. Belle is nothing like that man and you know it."

"Jess—" I began again.

She didn't let me go any further. "Don't be stupid. Don't ruin the best thing you found. I saw you with her. I knew you were falling for her. Think about it. If this is what you're going to do, you might as well just plan to spend the rest of your life alone. I get being upset with her, but at least give her a chance if you love her."

27

BELLE

"That's weird," I murmured to myself as I checked my phone calendar once more.

I scrolled back to the month before, checking to confirm when my last period was. "It's got to be a mistake."

I was home one night after work, and I was just now discovering I was late. For my period, that is. I was remarkably regular. I'd had a habit for years of marking it in my calendar on my phone whenever I got my period. I was late, for sure.

Lowering my hand, I swallowed, and my belly did a nervous revolution in my stomach. Ty and I had used condoms every time. My mind picked through my recollections. The problem was, every encounter with Ty was hot, like immolate-my-brain-cells hot. I knew we'd waited until the last second to deal with the condom more than once.

I was alone in my apartment, and I stood abruptly, walking in a tight circle around my living room. I knew I couldn't wait to figure this out until morning, so I grabbed my purse. A few minutes later when I pulled up to a jerking stop in front of the small shopping strip with the drugstore, I realized they were closed. Colebury wasn't Burlington where things tended to be open later. I aimed my car toward Montpelier. Maybe, just maybe, they would have a drugstore open at this hour.

I forced myself to use cruise control so I didn't speed. I tried to listen to music as a distraction, but it was impossible to keep my thoughts from running laps in my mind. I breathed a sigh of relief when I saw the open drugstore in a small shopping area. I dashed in, inexplicably buying three pregnancy tests. Just to make sure.

Roughly a half an hour later, I was back in my apartment, staring at the little stick I needed to put under my pee. I was almost afraid to do it, but I knew my anxiety was going to spiral if I didn't get an answer. Until then, I was panicking about the unknown.

A few minutes later, I had scrambled up the nerve and peed on two out of three sticks. That had taken a little maneuvering, but I pulled it off. Matters had been helped by the fact that I really had to pee.

I waited, forcing myself to walk out of the bathroom and pace in the living room. When I returned to the bathroom and saw both tests with distinct blue lines, I was completely frozen for a minute before I clapped my hands over my mouth when I almost screeched aloud. Although my elderly landlady didn't have the best hearing, I didn't want to startle her by screaming late at night.

Oh, fuck. I was pregnant. There was absolutely no doubt who the father was. I didn't know what the hell to do.

Ty had worked an evening shift tonight, and we'd hardly spoken since he broke things off. I was beyond relieved I had time to completely panic all by myself. Because I didn't think I could hide this from him, and I didn't know what to do.

The following morning, I woke early. I hadn't slept well, not even a little. I probably maybe got one full hour of sleep. Coffee at the Busy Bean was in order.

After a shower, I got dressed and blow dried my hair. Not because I was styling it, but because it was just chilly enough out that I didn't want to get cold on my short walk down there.

A little while later, I pushed through the door to the café and the bell above the door gave a cheery little jingle. I was surprised to see Zara at the register behind the counter. Usually, it was one of the baristas.

She looked a little tired, and I felt a spurt of kinship.

"Morning," she said, offering me a quick smile. "Coffee?"

I opened my mouth to order a coffee and stuttered on my own words. I slammed my mouth shut and then said, "I guess I'll have some herbal tea. What kind do you have?"

Zara regarded me quietly, and one dark brow rose. "Tea?" She paused, glancing to the side. "We don't even have it on the menu, but we have some just in case people ask. Let's see, we have raspberry tea, lemon tea, and a few others." I felt my cheeks get hot. "Is everything okay?" she pressed.

"I'm pregnant," I blurted out.

Zara met my announcement with a glance at her watch. "Let's get you some tea, and I'll sit with you," she said when she looked back at me. "It's only six, and Roderick's busy baking in the back. We don't get too many customers at this hour."

Next thing I knew, Zara was looking at me across a table moments later after prepping me a cup of tea and some coffee for herself. "You seem surprised," she commented.

"Well, I am. Trust me, this was *not* planned, and I'm totally freaking out. Is it that obvious?"

Her eyes were warm and understanding. "It isn't obvious that you're pregnant, just that you're freaking out. I might have some experience with unplanned pregnancy," she said dryly.

"Oh," I said slowly, recalling the story of Zara's secret when she first got pregnant.

Zara gave me a rueful smile. "Yep. Best thing that ever happened to me. But I didn't know it would turn out that way at first."

"I'm definitely freaking out," I said, taking a sip of my tea.

I stared down at the mug, a strange feeling of anticipation tightening in my chest. The fact that I'd even thought about whether or not I should have coffee or tea made me wonder if my subconscious already had a feeling about this. If I wasn't going to keep the baby, why would I even care if I had coffee?

Lifting my eyes, I met her understanding gaze. "What do you want to do?" she asked. Blessedly, she gave me a moment while she took a swallow of her coffee.

"I think if you had asked me yesterday morning if I found out I was accidentally pregnant, I probably would've told you that I thought I wouldn't plan on keeping it. I don't know what I want to do, but then maybe I do because I got herbal tea. Which totally isn't waking me up." I cast a glare at my tea, and Zara chuckled.

She took another swallow of her coffee, drumming her fingertips on the table after she set her mug down. "I suppose I had a similar view. I definitely didn't expect to get pregnant, and I couldn't find Dave. I was surprised at how quickly I knew I wanted to have Nicole though. Even when I didn't know she would be a girl, and when I didn't know she would practically be the spitting image of her father. Although, he swears she has my glare."

Zara rolled her eyes at that, and I managed to laugh. We fell quiet, and I took another sip of my tea, thinking I was probably going to get a headache because I wasn't going to get enough caffeine. I thought about the way Dave looked at Zara when I saw them together and experienced a sharp burning sensation over my heart. It almost stung, and I unconsciously rubbed my knuckles over it.

I wanted something like that—a man who was totally smitten with me, even after babies and toddlers and the messiness that could come along with them.

"I'm assuming you know who the father is," she said quietly.

I looked over, nodding quickly. "I've only had sex with one

guy in more than a year—Ty. We've always used condoms, but things got pretty hot and heavy at times."

"Are you going to tell him?"

That panic I'd been trying to hold at bay knotted tightly inside my chest as I looked over at her. I took a gulp of tea, closing my eyes and taking a breath after I swallowed.

Opening them, I took another breath before answering, "I think I have to, but he broke it off. What do you think I should do?"

"I think if you think you want to have this baby, you need to tell him. Same goes if you decide you don't want to have this baby, but you want a relationship with him, or frankly even a friendship. That's a massive secret to keep, no matter what you decide."

"Oh, my God." I uncurled my fingers from the mug handle and put my face in my hands. After several deep breaths, I lifted my head, letting my hands fall flat to the table. "I can't hide this, it just won't feel right."

Zara surprised me by reaching over and curling one of her hands over mine. Her grip was firm and her hand warm. She squeezed before releasing. "It will be fine. You're going to feel like you're flailing. No matter what. I got through it with a lot of help from my family until Dave came back to town. Even when they're planned, babies are not easy. It's definitely a fly by the seat of your pants life experience. For me, it's when I finally grew up. It seems like you've already walked through a fire or two in life."

Her observation made me wonder what she knew about me, but I didn't feel defensive. There was something about Zara, a clear-eyed lack of judgment about people. On the one hand, she would be quick to call someone out on their bullshit. On the other, she was kind and funny, and I sensed she'd faced her own challenges beyond what I knew.

The sense of panic spinning inside started to recede. I took a breath, letting it out before draining my tea. "Wish me luck then."

"You're going to tell him today?"

"I might as well. I'm not good at keeping secrets. I never was."

"Are you two serious?"

I sighed and shook my head. "I fucked up, and he broke it off."

"Pregnancy tends to be a defining experience. It'll be okay. You have my number, right?" she asked suddenly, just as another customer came into the café.

"I don't know." I lifted my phone, scrolling through my contacts. I shook my head.

Zara took my phone from me and quickly entered her number. "If you need to chat, just text me, and I'll call."

28

TY

It was late evening, and I was tired. I wanted nothing more than a few hours with Belle, tangled up skin to skin. Instead, I clomped up the stairs alone after spending an hour sanding the beams downstairs for the sole purpose of keeping myself distracted.

My phone vibrated in my pocket, and I slipped it out. The second I saw Belle's name on the message banner, I stopped at the top of the stairs.

I need to talk to you. Can I come by tonight?

Questions raced through my thoughts, but I was tired of missing her, so I acted on impulse. *Sure.*

She replied that she'd be on her way in a few. I was relieved I didn't have long to wait. I didn't know why she needed to talk to me, but I wanted to see her more than I wanted to wonder.

Moments after she arrived, it was obvious she was nervous. She was standing in the kitchen, her fingertips drumming restlessly on the counter.

I slid my hips onto a stool by the counter and spun to face her. I almost reached for her, but I caught myself.

When I looked over at her, an unfamiliar sense of protectiveness rose within me. Her face was pale, and her freckles stood out.

She seemed out of sorts, and I wanted to fix it for her even though I didn't know what was wrong.

The sound of her swallowing was audible as she looked up at me and blurted out, "I'm pregnant."

I blinked, not comprehending her words, even though there were only two of them. "What?"

She cleared her throat. "I'm pregnant. Obviously, I didn't expect this."

I simply kept staring blankly at her. "Are you sure?" I finally managed.

"I've taken three pregnancy tests. They all came back positive. I scheduled an appointment with the doctor next week."

My brain felt filled with static. "Uh, wow. I don't know what to think," I said, being flatly honest.

Belle's eyes were glistening, and she blinked rapidly. She cleared her throat again. "I understand. I'm not sure what I'm going to do."

I tried to get my brain into gear. It felt like a car that was almost starting, but cutting out before the engine caught. "Okay, I guess you should let me know how that goes."

I knew I wasn't handling this well, but I had *no* fucking idea how to handle this.

"What do you want?" she whispered, her voice frayed.

"I have no idea. I just need to wrap my brain around this," I said haltingly.

Belle nodded quickly and stepped back. "I'll go then."

Before I could even register what she was doing, she practically ran out of the barn. I heard her footsteps on the stairs, the sound echoing up to the landing because she left the door open behind her. Belatedly, I stood. I didn't want her to bolt like this.

I wasn't fast enough though. By the time I got downstairs and outside, the glow of her tail lights down the driveaway mocked me in the darkness.

Without thinking, I jogged to my truck, only to climb in and realize I didn't have my keys. "Fuck." I lightly bounced my fist on the steering wheel before hustling out and racing up the stairs.

As bad luck would have it, I couldn't find where I'd put my keys. It was only after fifteen minutes of searching the upstairs that I remembered to check downstairs.

The sound of my feet scuffing on the sawdust covered floor was only slightly louder than the static in my brain. I found my keys on the worktable. Spinning them on my forefinger, I rested my hips against the table and looked out the windows into the darkness.

The moon cast a pearly glow, illuminating a portion of the mountain range in the distance. The delay in searching for my keys had caused my racing thoughts to slow just enough that I knew I needed to be able to say something sensible before chasing after Belle.

"Fuck. She's pregnant." My raspy words were loud in the empty and dark space.

Fishing my phone out of my pocket, my thumbs hovered over the screen. I didn't even know what to text her. Yet, I felt pressed to say something.

I'm guessing my reaction wasn't great. I was shocked. I'm not sure what's best now. I'm here whenever you're ready to talk.

I hit send before I could chicken out. "Fuck." No matter what, I knew I needed to support whatever Belle wanted, and I was close to the edge of panic.

The static filling my thoughts was the only reason I answered when my phone vibrated, and I saw it was my father.

Before I could get a word in, he opened with, "Ty."

His tone was sharp, but then it was always sharp. Like he was half-paying attention and annoyed at the interruption, even when he happened to be the one who initiated the call.

"Hey, Dad."

There was a long silence and then I added, "I wasn't expecting your call."

"I didn't think you were."

I took a breath, marshaling my thoughts. I was determined not to fall into the stinging back and forth of most of our conversations.

I waited, and then he did the predictable. "I thought I'd try once again to ask you about working in the business."

"You're calling me now to ask this?" I prompted, more bitterly amused than angry.

"One of our VP's is relocating, so the timing seemed right."

I took a quiet breath as a strange sense of peace settled over me. I was feeling anything but peaceful about Belle, but oddly the crisis with her cast this situation with my father in sharp relief. "Stop, just fucking stop. I don't want to work for you, and that's not going to change."

After several beats of quiet, my father asked, "Did your sister put you up to this?"

I leaned my head back, gritting my teeth to keep from snapping. "No. In the past, she has suggested I tell you to fuck off. That's not what I'm doing. I'm asking you to stop pressuring me about work. We haven't had a good relationship, and I don't know if we ever will, but I'd like you to respect my answer about working with you as final."

"Ty—" my father began.

I cut him off at the pass of his question because I knew where this was going. "Dad, I don't want a lecture on why you think I'm making a bad decision. I'm not going to change my mind. If you keep asking, I'll stop answering your calls. My life is here now, and that's not changing."

He went quiet again before clearing his throat. "All right."

"I assume you'd like me to work for you because a part of you cares about me. I don't know how it will work out, but I'd like us to at least have a civil relationship. That won't happen if you're constantly badgering me whenever you call me."

"Fair enough," my father said slowly.

Now, to my next point. "Look, because I know how you operate, I can guess why you decided to look up Belle. I don't appreciate it. I care about her, and she matters to me." Maybe nothing was settled with me and Belle, maybe we weren't even together, but I had to say this to him.

A rustling sound carried through the line. "Okay. I hope you're not being foolish."

"It doesn't really matter if I am, Dad."

"I hope you can understand I'm just trying to protect your interests."

"Jesus, Dad. Belle is a decent person, and she doesn't deserve you digging into her background when you don't even have the context to understand. Nobody's perfect, not even you. Plenty of people know about your affair. If anyone wanted to make things awkward, they could."

My father snapped, "You wouldn't dare."

I sighed, tired of my father and his bullshit. "Dad, I don't want to spread any gossip, not because of you, but because of Mom. I think you get my point. You're not exactly a saint and Lord knows what else you've done that I don't know about. No one leads a perfect life. Some of us pay a steeper price than others for our mistakes." I paused, giving my father a chance to say something, but he stayed silent. "I'll talk to you later, and please don't call if you can't respect my wishes."

I waited a second and hung up, because I didn't sense my father would know how to respond right now. He would cogitate and ruminate and probably eventually respect my request. I doubted I'd ever have a great relationship with my dad, but I was weary of our petty bickering.

After that call, I realized all I'd ever needed to get me to the other side with my father was something much more important. Belle was pregnant, and I had no idea how to bridge the chasm I'd created before that news had been dropped like a bomb between us.

Restless, I found myself pacing. When that wasn't enough to dispel my edginess, I strode outside. I leaned my head back and looked up at the stars. They glittered bright and sharp against the inky black sky. In the quiet, I heard a soft mewling sound nearby and glanced around. I waited to see if I'd hear it again. It came again, and I thought it was coming from a small shed situated just beyond the back of the barn.

I walked slowly in that direction. Another mewl reached my ears when I got close to the shed. There was enough light cast from the light above the door that I could see a pair of eyes gleaming underneath the shed. I knelt and took a closer look to see a kitten hiding there. When I held a hand out, the kitten scurried further back. The nights were getting colder, and I wasn't sure how long this kitten could survive on its own outside.

"Hey there," I murmured.

When the kitten stayed put, I rose and walked inside. I fetched two plastic containers out of a cabinet, pouring milk in one. After some deliberation, I opened a can of tuna and put some in the other container. I had no idea what was best to feed a kitten, but I'd have to go to the store tomorrow to get some food if the kitten was still there tomorrow morning.

After I left the milk and tuna just under the edge of the shed while the kitten's glittering eyes tracked me, I returned inside and called the only person I could think to call as I walked back upstairs and plopped down on the couch.

"Hey, Ty," my sister said in her jaunty voice. "What are you doing calling me so late at night? You know, I could be busy."

"Are you?"

Jess was quiet for a beat, her voice softer when she replied, "No, but based on how you sound, if I was, I'd cancel my plans. What's wrong?"

"Belle's pregnant."

Jess must've taken a sip of something, because she sputtered before saying, "Dammit. I got water on my keyboard. Hang on."

In another second, she was back. "Okay, what the hell? She's pregnant? Are you sure it's yours?"

"Absolutely." There might be things I doubted, but that detail wasn't one of them.

"Wow," Jess said slowly. "Do you know what she plans to do?"

I kicked my feet up on the coffee table where I was sitting on my couch, running a hand through my hair with a sigh. "Unfortunately, no. She just told me tonight. I was kind of shocked, and she bolted."

"I'm sure she's shocked too," Jess pointed out.

"Oh, yeah. That much is clear."

"Okay, are you calling for support, or feedback, or both?"

My laugh was dry, and I didn't quite feel it. But I appreciated Jess's question. We'd established that habit with each other when we used to call and vent about whatever. Sometimes one or the other of us wanted advice, and sometimes we just wanted to bitch and have someone say, "Yeah, I get it."

"I don't really know."

"Okay." My sister took on her practical tone, as I liked to call it. I could imagine her rolling her sleeves up. "Obviously, this is a big deal. You need to support whatever she wants to do. You know, it's her body, her choice, and all that jazz."

"You don't have to talk me into that, I'm on board."

"Well, if she wants to keep the baby, how do you feel about that?"

"That's the million-dollar question. I've had less than an hour to ponder this."

"What's your gut reaction?"

"You mean beyond the panic?"

Jess's laugh was warm and understanding and that tight feeling in my chest started to loosen. "Yes, beyond the panic."

"I don't know. It's not that I'm opposed to having a baby, but I sure as hell wasn't planning on it. Not that you asked, but we've been using condoms."

"I'm sure you have," Jess said dryly. "And that, frankly, is more than I wanted to know about your sex life."

This time, my laugh was genuine. I still felt as if I were floundering, like someone had tossed me in the ocean and I couldn't see land. Somehow, I had to figure out where it was.

"If you haven't already, you need to call her and tell her you're there for her however she needs you to be there for her. The last time we talked, you'd broken things off with her. Did you do anything about that since?"

Jess just *had* to go and ask that. Her question felt like a stinging dart right into the center of my heart. Every time I thought about Belle and scrambling up the courage to repair the rupture between us, I felt something like the feral kitten I'd discovered hiding outside tonight—uncertain who to trust. Just like when I got close to the kitten and it backed away, trying to make itself invisible. That was like my mind when I tried to contemplate the enormity of my feelings for Belle. Holy hell, I needed to get a grip.

"I told you I love her, but we haven't patched things up yet," I finally said.

"Well, that's dumb," Jess countered quickly. "This is a pretty heavy thing to go through without you having the nerve to talk to her."

"I talked to her tonight," I muttered.

"Because she told you she was pregnant!" my sister practically screeched.

Because there was no solving this for now, I tried to deflect. "I found a kitten under the shed."

"You did?"

"I just said I did."

"Is it okay?"

"I couldn't see very well, but I hope so. I took some milk and tuna out. Hopefully, I can bribe it out soon."

"You better keep checking on it," Jess ordered.

"I will. I swear," I insisted.

"Keep me posted. Now, back to your situation. You are going to have to dig deep and get over yourself with this."

So much for deflection. "Calling you is supposed to make me feel better."

Jess sighed. "I hope it does, a little. But I can't wrap this up in platitudes for you. If you love Belle, you need to do something about it."

"I will," I said, my tone low. I didn't know how yet, but I would.

Maybe my sister didn't solve anything, but she did nudge me in the right direction. I'd already known I missed Belle too much. It had cut deep when I realized she hadn't trusted me enough to tell me the whole truth, but she mattered too much to let her slip away.

Before I went to bed, I went outside to check on the kitten. That pair of eyes watched me carefully, but it didn't inch any closer. The tuna was gone, along with most of the milk though.

I didn't sleep well that night, and Belle never replied to my text.

BELLE

"Honey," my mother's voice came through the bathroom door. "Can I get you anything?"

Apparently, I was one of the unlucky ones who got morning sickness early. I'd had to race to the bathroom when I woke up, just barely making it to the toilet to empty what little I had in my stomach. Then, my mother made me a nice bowl of oatmeal with maple syrup and butter.

My stomach didn't like that either, and I was eyeing the pretty blue tiles on the floor as I rested my cheek against the cool surface of the toilet seat. After a moment, I wiped my mouth with a tissue, flushed the toilet and splashed cold water on my face after I washed my hands. Glancing at myself in the mirror, I was greeted with the sight of my pale skin and bleary eyes. To top it all off, I'd slept like shit, and my mother had questions.

I figured I might as well face the music. On the heels of a deep breath, I walked out. My mother blinked at me. "Do you have a stomach bug?"

"No," I said flatly. "And, if you're worried I was out partying, I wasn't. I don't have a hangover."

My mother trailed behind me as I walked down the hall and returned to the kitchen. I could practically hear her chewing on the insides of her cheeks to keep from bombarding me with polite questions. My parents tried awfully hard not to press me too much ever since my night in the hospital. I knew it had hurt them when I refused to let one of their legal friends help clean up my situation. For some reason, that detail had been very important to me. I needed to take care of things my way and on my terms. Since the attorney at the pro bono program had helped me, the program had subsequently gotten a generous donation from my parents. I'd only heard about that from May after the fact.

Because I was feeling defensive and, frankly, drained, I decided to launch into that topic when we sat back down at the kitchen table. Blessedly, my father was at the office.

"You know, Mom, you could've told me you donated that money to the legal program that helped me."

My mother cocked her head to the side. "Do you really want to argue about that now, Belle? It was a perfectly worthy donation, and it's an excellent program."

Jesus. It was nearly impossible to stay angry at my mother because she was so freaking reasonable. "Well, I can't argue with that," I muttered.

"Honey, what's wrong? I'm trying not to be too concerned, but you showed up unexpectedly and you don't seem well."

"Before you worry about this, I'm not having a manic episode." I gestured vaguely in the air for no particular reason.

"It doesn't seem like that. Perhaps we haven't mentioned it, but your father and I met with a therapist."

"You met with my therapist?" I squeaked.

"Oh, no! Before you worry, our marriage is fine, but we felt like we needed to have a good understanding of what you went through and the details we missed. We also talked more with my sister. It's been very helpful. Now, we understand that when you start buzzing like a little bee, that maybe we need to pay better attention." I snorted at that description, and my mother cast me a quick smile. "You're not buzzing like a bee. You weren't last night when you got here, and you're sick this morning. Would you like some ginger tea?"

"That would be nice." As soon as she suggested it, I knew that might help settle my stomach.

My mother stood to set the kettle on the stove and fetch two mugs.

"I'm pregnant," I announced, lobbing that little news bomb into the silence.

I heard my mother's sharp intake of breath. To her credit, she didn't turn around yet. She filled the kettle with water, set it on the stove and turned on the burner before getting out two teabags, ginger for me and English breakfast for her, because that was her favorite.

When she sat back down, she had a pinched look that I knew well. She was silently freaking out inside and trying not to let it show.

"It's okay, you can totally freak out. I did," I assured her.

"Well, I certainly wasn't expecting this. Is this morning sickness then? How long have you known?"

"Two days. Based on my math, I should be about five weeks along."

I'd done some guesswork based on my last period and one of the times Ty and I waited until the very last second before he put a condom on. I was able to narrow it to a date because it was after a late night at work when we had an event at the restaurant. We'd both been wired from the rush of an insanely busy night and burned off that energy with each other. I was the one who straddled him and teased him by sliding over the underside of his cock. I didn't think my mother needed all *that* detail though.

My mother took a deep breath and let it out in a controlled sigh. "We'll support you however you like. What do you plan to do?"

It seemed like I *should* have a plan. I had *no* freaking plan. *This* wasn't planned. The only thing I knew was a pretty big part of my heart, all but maybe one small corner, really wanted this baby.

And yet, I was ashamed at how much I was panicking and worried that it was a disastrous decision for me to make.

I traced my fingertip along the curved handle of my mug. I felt tears pricking at the backs of my eyes and blinked before finally lifting my gaze to meet my mother's.

"I think I want to keep the baby," I said softly.

I waited, bracing myself for her to tell me why this wasn't a good decision. The last few years of my life were littered with the debris of my bad decisions. There was my bad relationship, which blessedly my parents didn't know a whole lot about. It hadn't been horrible, but it had felt like I was walking a balance beam, one day after another where I stumbled and my ex lashed out at me. Thank God he wanted nothing to do with me after my arrest and the inglorious pinnacle of my manic episode. That and me dropping out of law school, not even trying to stay in school when they had assured me there was a chance to work things out.

I vividly remembered the look on my parents faces when they came to pick me up at the hospital. It was some combination of worried, concerned, horrified, and epically disappointed.

My mother was quiet, her eyes soft as she regarded me from across the table. "If that's what you want, that's what you should do."

I was so startled, my mouth dropped open slightly. My mother's lips curled in a rueful smile. "Were you expecting a lecture from me?"

"Not a lecture, per se, but maybe a few reminders about how I haven't made the best decisions in the last few years."

My mother's smile faded and she leaned forward, resting her elbows on the table. "Actually, I think you've made some really good decisions. You have faced challenges that most people don't ever have to face. Maybe it didn't play out the way you would've liked, but you found your path. If everything hadn't happened the way it did, I think you would've gone into law and probably never quite found peace for yourself. I know you really love being a chef, and I'm so happy you found that."

I felt all choked up, a sudden rush of emotion cresting inside. I didn't realize I'd actually started to cry until my mother handed me a napkin from the small stack they always kept on the kitchen table. After I wiped my tears, I curled the napkin in my hand and looked over at her. "You really think so? I thought I'd let you and Dad down."

My mother sighed, pressing her lips together. "You can't let us down. We can be worried and concerned, and we can want what we think is best for you, but you'll never let us down. I'm not going to lie and pretend we weren't shocked and frightened when you got arrested and ended up in the hospital. I imagine you can understand that."

I'd gotten a hold of my tears and managed to laugh. "I was shocked and frightened, so yes, I can definitely understand," I offered in between sniffles.

"You always were the little girl who tried to please everyone. Whether we planted that seed or not, you wanted to please us and thought it would please us if you went into law. If that had been your passion, of course, we would've been thrilled. I don't think it was. You're so bright that it was easy for you to follow along that path. Some people might have struggled more, but you didn't and you enjoyed school."

"Not chemistry, I hated chemistry," I said.

My mother chuckled. "And yet, you still got an A."

I sighed, twisting my lips to the side. "True."

"You're very good at coming up with your own recipes for baking, which is a form of chemistry."

"Fine," I muttered with a dry laugh. My laugh stopped suddenly. "But a baby? I wasn't planning on a baby. Am I crazy to even consider having it?"

"People have been having babies they didn't plan on since the beginning of time," my mother pointed out calmly. "I think you have to ask yourself what you want. It would be good to know what the father wants. You're fully capable of being a single mother, but it's important to know. Are you comfortable telling me who the father is? Do you have a relationship with him?"

Oh Jesus, now we were talking about relationships. Fuck my life.

"I don't know if he wants the baby. I don't even know what our status is. We, uh, were taking a break. I might've told him about getting pregnant and then left in a rush."

"You might've?"

"Okay, that's what I did," I fessed up. "I panicked. He seemed really shocked."

"Is he a good man?"

I nodded quickly. "Absolutely." I knew Ty was a good man down to my bones.

"Perhaps you should talk to him again," my mother pointed out the obvious. "What does he do?"

"He's a manager at Speakeasy."

"Ah, sort of an office romance," my mother said, her lips quirking into a smile.

"We actually knew each other in college. He played hockey at Burlington University."

"Were you romantically involved then? You didn't exactly keep us up to speed on your relationships when you were in college."

My cheeks were hot. "Well, I didn't get serious with anyone. He was a nice guy back then too." That was all I was offering about that. I wasn't about to get into my hot nights with Ty, not with my mother.

"We'll support whatever you do. You know that."

"How do you think Dad will react?"

"He'll be surprised, but he'll be fine. We just want what's best for you. I really hope this man is not like your last boyfriend," my mother said, choosing her words carefully.

"He's not. I promise. Maybe I don't know what he wants as far as dealing with a surprise pregnancy, but I know he's a good man."

My mother took a swallow of her tea, angling her head to the side as she set her mug down. "Should we keep talking about this, or not?"

"I just need time to think."

If only I knew what Ty was thinking. I couldn't believe this had happened. There were surprises, and then there were things like this. No matter my decision, it was permanent.

30

——

TY

——

I tapped the play button on Belle's message again:

"Hey Ty, it's Belle. I got your text. I'm at my parents' house in Burlington. I just needed a few days. I know you said for me to let you know when I wanted to talk. I'm ready whenever you are. Obviously, this is a surprise for both of us. We have some things to figure out, but I don't want to force anything on you. I'll be back soon."

Her message ended, and I set my phone down on my kitchen counter, staring at it like it was a ticking time bomb. I needed her to come back to town so we could talk. It had been two full days since she dropped her news on me. I'd tried twice to call her, both times not leaving a message because I didn't know what the hell to say.

As I stared at the phone, it vibrated, a text banner showing on the screen. Glancing down, I saw it was from Griff. "Fuck," I muttered. I was late. I promised him I'd meet him at Speakeasy early to help with something in the brewing area.

I typed out a reply.

Sorry, running late. On the way.

As I was leaving, I caught sight of the stray kitten dashing from the side of the barn toward the shed. I was already late, but I couldn't leave without making sure to put out food. Jogging back upstairs, I returned with a small plastic bowl of canned food. I rinsed and filled a bowl of water under the spigot outside the barn entrance. Yep, that's how ridiculous I was getting over this kitten. I'd even gone to the store to get some food. I left the bowls in the usual spot under the edge of the shed.

Dust kicked up behind my truck as I sped down the gravel driveway. A short while later, I came to a jerking stop in the parking lot and jogged into Speakeasy. It was early, early enough that the only people here were Phoebe puttering in the kitchen, the new events coordinator Rosalie, and Griffin and Audrey.

When I entered the brewing room, Audrey was standing with hands on hips watching as Griffin fiddled with something. "Sorry I'm late," I called as I crossed the room.

Audrey cast me a warm smile over her shoulder as I approached. "Good morning. Griffin's only a little grumpy that you're late. He wouldn't have even needed you if I had longer arms." She held out her arms, as if in demonstration of this fact.

"Well, I guess it's always good to feel needed," I replied lightly.

Griffin straightened and patted two kegs. "I just wanna get these on the shelf over there." He pointed to the corner.

"Let's do it."

After we got the kegs moved, Griffin immediately moved along to check on something on one of the brewing tanks.

"Do you know when Belle will be back?" Audrey asked.

Tension gathered in my shoulders instantly. I wanted to know exactly when Belle would be back, and I needed to talk to her. Yet, I had no idea beyond her message that she'd be back soon. That left a lot of wiggle room. "I'm not sure," I replied, striving to keep my tone nonchalant.

"Is that why you're so distracted?" Griffin interjected.

"Come again?" I glanced to him.

"Dude, you were late this morning, and you're never late. You also spaced that meeting yesterday. Is there a problem?"

Audrey looked at me, her gaze unabashedly curious.

I stuffed my hands in my pockets, rolling my head side to side to ease the tension bundling in my neck. "Nope, no problem."

"In case you missed the memo, your secret's not so secret anymore," Audrey offered.

I bit back a groan. Meanwhile, Griffin gave me a sort of glowering look.

"I don't give a damn if you and her have a thing going," Griffin added. "However, I do give a damn if it interferes with work. We're not far past the other side of getting this place off to a good start. We need you focused and on point."

"Geez," Audrey interjected. "If Ty's a little distracted because he's in love with Belle, I'm sure it'll pass."

I practically choked. "What?" I sputtered.

Audrey gave me an understanding look, like I was a little slow. "It's obvious to me." With that she patted me on my arm, as if to comfort me. She then pinned her gaze on her husband. "Just because he missed one meeting doesn't mean he's distracted. Plus, not everyone's a morning person like you, farmer boy."

That elicited a chuckle from Griff, and she slipped her hand in the crook of his elbow. Just when I thought I was in the clear, Audrey glanced over once more. "Get your head on straight, or you're going to lose an awesome woman."

She waved over her shoulder while they walked out. I remained frozen in the center of the room for no particular reason other than the fact that I couldn't think straight. The mere suggestion I could lose Belle had panic clenching a cold fist around my heart.

Later that morning, I ran into Dave Beringer, at the grocery store of all fucking places. His cart was filled to overflowing, and I glanced down, asking, "Feeding a team?"

He laughed. "Yes, my family. How's it hanging?"

"Fine." When I glanced back up after grabbing a box of pasta and putting it in my basket, I ran into his gaze, sharp and assessing. "What?" I asked.

"Nothing," Dave replied blandly.

Next thing I knew, I asked him a ridiculous question. "What do you think of being a father?"

Dave's lips twitched, just a little. "Zara mentioned Belle had a surprise. I'm guessing she told you about it based on your question."

I nodded. "I have no fucking idea what to do."

Dave nodded, his gaze sympathetic. "By the time I found out I had a kid, Nicole was already a toddler. I completely panicked. Once I got used to the idea, having a kid is the best thing that ever happened for me. I like it so much that we have two now." He chuckled, before sobering quickly. "Trust me, I didn't plan on being a father. My childhood wasn't exactly great. Maybe you're shocked, but you're a decent guy. Parenting is way harder than hockey, but you learn on the fly, and that's not so bad. The effort definitely counts." He glanced down at his watch. "I gotta bolt. I need to be back to the house in time so Zara can get to work. Catch you later." He patted me on the shoulder. "Call me if you need anything."

I was left in the aisle at the grocery store, staring at his retreating back. I returned to work, grateful I could at least stay busy.

When I rolled down my driveway that night, it was late. Not because I technically had to work late. But I missed Belle, and it was Friday.

Even though Lily was handling the bar with help from RD at Speakeasy, and they hadn't needed me, there was always something to do. I'd holed up in the office and plowed through organizing our upcoming orders for the month. Griffin wanted me to be on point, so it only made sense to stay this late. It had nothing to do with missing Belle, or that's what I told myself.

Of course, staying late had turned out to be a mistake. A customer had dropped a glass, and I'd gone to help clean up since the bar was so busy. In the midst of it, I'd managed to get a nasty gash on my hand. Then, I'd had to clean the blood up and head to the closest walk-in clinic to get stitches. I hadn't been in the mood to deal with anyone coming with me and somehow the whole mess had me missing Belle even more. Everything did.

I carefully flexed my hand. The bandage was along the pad of my thumb, and the pain was reduced to a dull ache.

My mind spun back to Griffin's comments. Much as I hated to admit it, I knew he was right. I had spaced on that meeting because I wasn't thinking clearly. I was all up in my own head over Belle. I couldn't really wrap my brain around the fact that she was pregnant.

Oddly, although I could admit to some panic about it, there was a part of me that liked the idea. Oh, for sure, I was terrified of being a parent. But I liked the idea of being committed to Belle and making a life with her. Hell, I'd already fallen so hard for her. There was no sense in avoiding that. I'd never forgotten those nights with her before simply because they were so good.

We were still incredible together in bed. It was just easy, and the chemistry took over. But it wasn't only that. I also liked her and loved her. For a guy who never expected to find love, every time that word feathered along the edges of my thoughts, I dashed away.

I laughed as I realized the path of my thoughts reminded me of the kitten. I still didn't know if it was a boy or a girl. I'd taken to calling the kitten Silver. There was a bite to the cold air tonight as I climbed out of my truck. We'd had a frost more than one night, and I knew winter was waiting in the wings to chase autumn away.

My boots crunched on the gravel as I crossed over toward the shed. I could see Silver's eyes shining in the darkness. I approached slowly, kneeling down at a safe distance.

"Hey there," I murmured, holding my good hand out.

I'd persuaded Silver to approach for a few pets, but the second I'd tried to pick the kitten up, it dashed away. I was hoping I could at least get it inside. The nights were cold and getting colder.

Silver cautiously approached, sniffing my hand before darting away. It didn't dart all the way out of sight, and that gave me a little hope.

"Come on," I said, keeping my voice low and easy.

This time, Silver came a little closer, letting out a throaty purr when I scratched my fingers under its chin. When the kitten didn't bolt, I moved smoothly, scooping it up in my arms. The little kitten froze, but it didn't wiggle away, so I stood, feeling my heart pinch a little when I realized it was shivering.

"I told you it was getting cold." I spoke conversationally as I crossed over to the barn.

I was surprised to find a box tucked inside the entryway downstairs. It was a delivery that I wasn't expecting, so I didn't know what it was. I nudged it out of the way with my boot before jogging upstairs.

Once we were safely inside, I did a quick inspection and discovered the kitten was a girl. I carried her over to the kitchen counter. With one hand, I opened a can of kitten food and filled a small plastic container with some milk. I didn't know if kittens actually needed milk, but she sure liked it.

I figured that would keep her occupied while I went down and fetched the box. A minute later, I jogged back upstairs, eyeing the label on the box. It came from a major online retailer, but I still didn't know what the hell it was. As I hoped, Silver was occupied eating.

When I set the box down on the counter nearby, she looked over at me, but kept on eating her food. I used my keys to punch the tape open on the box. There was a card inside that said "A Gift for You". When I opened the small card, it said, "From Jess. In case you catch the kitten."

I'd taken a photo of Silver hiding under the shed the other day and texted it to her, telling her I was trying to catch the kitten. I laughed to myself. "Perfect timing."

Jess had sent me a bag of cat food, a few toys for the kitten, along with a litter box and the litter to go in it. I lifted my phone, snapping a quick picture of the kitten and the opened box, both of which I texted to my sister, saying, "It's a girl."

Seconds later, my phone rang. I tapped the speaker button and answered. "Hey there."

"Oh, my God! You caught her tonight!"

"Sure did. She's eating. Hang on, let me call you back on video." I switched over to the video screen to return the call and angled the screen so she could see Silver.

"Awww, she's so cute. You're sure she's a she."

I laughed. "I think so, but let's check again. Hang on." I set the phone down. I took a few steps closer to Silver. She'd just finished her bowl of food. It was only a half a can, and I needed to figure out portions. I held my hand out, and she didn't hesitate, immediately sniffing it before letting me pet her. She seemed to have decided I was safe. It was also warm in here, and I'd just fed her.

I lifted her up and turned her over in my arms, saying to Jess, "She's still a girl."

"What're you gonna name her?"

"I've been calling her Silver, and I think I'm going to keep that name."

"Do it. It's perfect. Her color's all swirly and silver."

"Thanks for thinking ahead. I hadn't even thought to get a litter box."

I shifted Silver in my hands, and Jess gasped. "What happened to your hand?"

I held it up. "No big deal. I cut it cleaning up some glass at work."

"Did you have to get stitches?"

"Yeah, but it'll be fine."

"You went by yourself to get stitches, didn't you?"

Rolling my eyes, I shrugged. "Why does it matter?"

"You're such a guy. Make sure to keep it clean." My sister sighed. "Back to Silver, are you going to let her run loose?"

"She's been living outside, Jess. I don't feel right keeping her inside all the time. I'll keep her in tonight, but I'll bring her downstairs tomorrow to see if she wants to go out."

"Something could eat her." Jess sounded affronted by my plan.

"True, but she's pretty savvy. She's been keeping herself safe all this time."

My sister grumbled. "Well, make sure you put food outside for her too."

"I will. I think she'll come back. This is a luxury step up for her."

She laughed softly. "All right. Let's be optimistic. Meanwhile, have you talked to Belle?"

Of course, Jess would go right to the sorest possible topic.

"No," I said, even though I didn't want to tell her the truth. "I tried twice to call her, and she left me a message. If I don't hear from her by tomorrow, I'll try again."

"What do you want, Ty?" Jess asked quietly.

"I'm not sure about the baby, but I know I love Belle," I finally said, the word feeling a little funny in my mouth even though I'd already admitted it.

"You sure about that?"

"Absolutely. Whatever Belle wants, I'll support. Trust me, I'm probably gonna lose my fucking shit if she wants to have this baby. I want to be with her, so it will be trial by fire, that's for sure."

BELLE

Laura drummed her fingertips on the arm of her chair. She was giving me a look I had come to know well. I knew she was about to call me on my bullshit. I just wasn't sure what bullshit was on the menu today.

"So, you're going back to Colebury, and you're worried that bolting from your job and your boyfriend—" I opened my mouth to clarify, and she held a finger up. "I'm calling him your boyfriend because that's what he is."

Sometimes it was uncomfortable how easily my therapist could read my mind. I'd been about to correct her that I wasn't sure what he was to me, but I pressed my lips together and held my silence.

"None of what you've done over the last few days has anything to do with you having Bipolar Disorder. You told your boss you needed a few days off. Most people who don't expect to be pregnant tend to panic about it. Hell, even people who have kids and are open to the idea of having more might be a little startled. Cut yourself some slack. I can't say that enough. You hold yourself to a standard no one can meet. It's okay to be a little scared."

Her voice gentled as she held my gaze. I suddenly wanted to

cry. So, I did. Because if you didn't feel safe crying in front of your therapist, you might want to find a new one.

She handed me the always conveniently placed box of tissues and let me cry for a minute. The rush of emotion passed quickly. I wiped my eyes and blew my nose. "Okay, so I'm not being stupid?" I finally asked.

"No, not at all. It's great to take things in stride, but some surprises are truly enormous. I'm also going to take the liberty of guessing that Ty was shocked and that's why his response was so flat. That doesn't mean he doesn't want to have a baby, or doesn't want to go through this process with you. But it's big, it's really big."

"I know. He's called me twice since I left him a message. He didn't leave a message, so I don't know what that means."

"Maybe it just means he'd like to discuss this face-to-face. Voicemails and texts suck for difficult topics. Before you go thinking he should've come and found you, he doesn't know where your parents live, and it might be a little stalker-ish if he did that."

I laughed and blew my nose again. "Maybe so. Well, I'm going back. I have a job, and I don't want to be a flake."

"You're not a flake, Belle. Telling your boss you had a personal emergency is what responsible people do."

I took a shaky breath, scrambling up my nerve. "Is it a bad decision to have a baby when I know it's possible a child of mine could inherit the genetic trait for Bipolar from me? And, what about my medication?"

"I'll start with your medication: talk to your doctor. There are lots of women taking medication for a variety of things that they need to adjust or manage when they're pregnant."

I took a breath and nodded. "Right. I'll talk to my doctor. I can do that."

"To your other concern, you could *not* have Bipolar Disorder and have a child that ended up with the diagnosis, just like your parents. Yes, there's a branch on your family tree with that trait, but lots of people don't even know things like that. They might have a relative who's hypomanic for years and that's all that ever happens. There might not be a genetic trait and you could have the first baby who adds the trait to the family tree. There's always a chance. There are so many things that could happen for a child. It's destructive to try to think like that. You're a caring, loving human being who has already been through some shit in life, so you're more qualified than many parents."

"What do you think I should do?" I swallowed through the emotion thick in my throat. I *really* wanted someone to tell me what to do and promise it would be the right thing to do.

Laura's gaze was calm and warm. "Life is hard, and I can't make you any guarantees or promises. I also can't tell you what to do. We've already covered the fact that you want this baby, so go back and talk to your man about it."

"Oh, now he's my man?"

"Yes," she said with a sly smile. "I don't know, obviously, but my gut tells me he wants to be with you. So, go figure it out." She glanced at the clock above the door. "Our time's about up."

I stood from my chair, smoothing my hands over my skirt. "Thanks for fitting me in. I'll be heading back to Colebury tomorrow."

"Look at that, your emergency will be a total of four days. No big deal."

I took a shaky breath. "I know, but I left abruptly so I feel bad."

"There's always the option to tell your boss what happened. I'm sure she'll understand. Shit happens for everybody. I think we should plan on an appointment next week, okay?"

"You were going to have to beat me away with a stick if we didn't schedule," I replied earnestly.

I had texted Phoebe that I'd be back tomorrow, but I was still nervous. I recalled my therapist pointing out it was only four days. But, still. The state of panic when I left had me worried that somehow I'd screwed things up.

Early that evening, I was in my childhood bedroom packing my single backpack when my phone chirped on the dresser. Crossing over to check on it, I saw a text from May.

Not sure if you're back in town yet. Did you hear about Ty getting hurt?

Panic slammed into me. I fumbled and dropped my phone. When I tried to call May, she didn't answer, and I swore. The doubts and uncertainty I'd been swimming in dissolved instantly. All I knew was I needed to get to Ty. I stuffed the last few things in, grabbed my backpack off the bed and ran down the stairs.

My parents were in the living room. I must've looked wild when I stopped in the archway from the hall. "I have to go. Ty got hurt."

My mother stood. "Is he okay?"

"I don't know, but I'm going back to Colebury tonight."

They must've realized I wasn't about to wait, so they hugged me goodbye and asked me to call with an update.

Moments later, I was on the highway heading for Colebury. Only then did I call May again.

"Is Ty okay?" I barked out as soon as she answered.

"He cut himself cleaning up some glass at Speakeasy last night. He's fine, but he did have to get stitches," she said quickly.

"How bad is it?" I pressed.

"Not that bad, but I haven't seen him."

I was sort of relieved and sort of pissed off. "Your text was vague enough to freak me right out," I muttered. "I tried to call you right away."

"I saw that, but right after I texted you Alec called. Are you coming back soon?"

"I'm on my way now, but how did you even know I was gone?"

"Did you forget how small this town is?" she asked wryly.

"Well, I know, but it's only been a few days."

"That's forever in this town," she teased.

I took a breath. "God, I hope I didn't screw things up too badly. It was an emergency," I offered, rather sheepishly.

"I'm sure it's fine. Life happens."

I suspected May might know what I had shared with Zara, but I had no way of knowing if she did. "I'm pregnant," I finally offered.

"Ah, now that's some news," she said, all casual like it was no big deal. "How are you handling it?"

"It's crazy, and my life feels like a hot mess."

"I wouldn't describe your life as a hot mess. In fact, except for Ty, you're busy with work and otherwise living a boring life."

"Okay, when you say it like that, sure. But I wasn't planning on getting pregnant, and I'm pretty sure Ty wasn't planning on me getting pregnant either. Actually, I know he wasn't. We used condoms every time."

"Accidents happen and all that. What do you want to do?"

She was so calm that it almost annoyed me. "It feels like I have to decide soon. Because I do. I would've liked to maybe have planned this. But I didn't." I swallowed. "Maybe it's totally crazy but I want this baby, and I have no idea how Ty's going to react to that."

"How did he react when you told him you were pregnant?"

"He didn't say much, and then I bolted."

"But you're on the way back," she said matter-of-factly.

I sighed. "From an objective perspective, how much of a mess is my life?"

"I understand how you're feeling. You were kind of a hot-shot before. From the outside, you had your shit together. If there's one thing I've figured out, it's that everybody feels like a mess sometimes. All you can do is keep going. You've already been through something really hard, and you landed on your feet. If you want this baby, then that choice is yours to make. I don't know what Ty thinks, obviously, but he's a good guy. I'm guessing he'll be there for you. What do you want with him?"

Oh geez, May was going to make me cry. My heart felt a piercing ache. The thing was, I'd already fallen so hard for Ty, and I wanted a chance for us. I was afraid having a baby was going to blow that chance to pieces unless he wanted our baby too. I knuckled away my tears with one hand and took a shuddery breath.

"Oh, hon," May said warmly. "It'll be okay. I'm pretty sure he feels the same way. I'm not sure about the baby part, but I think he's got it bad for you."

"How do you know?" I croaked. I gripped the steering wheel and kept my eyes focused on the road.

"Just a feeling. Plus, Alec thinks Ty's in love with you."

"Oh, God. Is this something people are gossiping about?"

"Not really. Okay, maybe a little," she corrected.

I groaned, and May laughed softly. "You've got this. I know you can handle it. Plus, Ty is cute, so there's that."

I swiped at my tears with one hand and let out a shaky laugh. Somehow, May found the perfect balance of support and lightness I needed.

"I'm thinking your text earlier was deliberately vague."

May's sly laugh had me shaking my head. "I thought you needed a nudge. I saw Ty earlier today and he looked sad. I think he misses you."

The drive wasn't too long, and I aimed straight for Ty's place.

32

BELLE

Ty's truck wasn't there when I stopped at his barn. I'd toyed with texting him to let him know I was coming, but I decided against it. I was feeling too emotional to try to find him at Speakeasy. The last thing I needed was to fall apart in front of everyone at work.

I fished the key out of the empty flower box he'd shown me before and made my way upstairs. Once I closed the door behind me upstairs, I was startled to discover a pretty silver kitten dashing across the floor. The kitten circled my feet as I toed off my shoes and hung up my jacket. Completely charmed, I lifted the kitten into my arms a moment later.

"Hey, you," I murmured, savoring the sound of her rumbling purr.

I didn't know when Ty got this little kitten, but the fact he had her gave me a burst of optimism. If he could take care of a kitten, maybe he would want our baby.

It wasn't long before I saw the arc of Ty's headlights in the windows as he parked at the end of the driveway.

A moment later, Ty came walking upstairs. I'd stood and walked over to the kitchen counter. The door clicked shut behind him, and we stared at each other. My heart started hammering hard in my chest, and my breath seized in my lungs for a moment.

I waited, expecting him to look—I didn't know what—angry, annoyed, panicked, or something else not good.

"Hey, Belle," he finally said. His lips kicked up in a crooked grin, and my heart gave a little peculiar thump.

"Hey," I returned, my lips tugging into a smile. "I hope it's okay I let myself in."

"It's fine. I'm glad you're back," he said quietly.

I nodded, and I suddenly wanted to cry, not bad tears or sad tears, it was just a rush of emotion so abrupt that tears were the only thing that went with it. I managed to breathe through it and didn't fall to pieces.

His eyes bored into mine for a moment, the look there so intense it took my breath away.

His gaze sobered after a moment, and the enormity of what we were facing hit me. My heartbeat stuttered and then lunged. "It'll be okay, Belle," he said, somehow knowing I needed to hear that specifically from him.

The moment ended when I noticed the bandage on his hand. I set the kitten down, hurrying over to him. "May told me you cut your hand. Are you okay?"

I reached for his hand, and he let me inspect the bandage. Not that there was much to see other than a tidy piece of gauze taped in place. When my eyes bounced up to his, he explained, "I was cleaning up glass at the bar. The stitches are the dissolvable kind. I promise I'm fine. A little ibuprofen is enough for the pain."

I nodded, glancing away when the kitten's motion distracted me. "Your kitten's really cute."

His chuckle spun around my heart and sent goosebumps prickling over the surface of my skin. It seemed no matter how heavy the pending topic might be, Ty could still turn me on effortlessly.

He cast me a lopsided smile just as the little ball of silver fluff came dashing over. He leaned down in one smooth motion and scooped up the kitten. "Hey there, Silver," he greeted the kitten conversationally. He looked to me. "She's a girl."

She batted at his cheek with one of her tiny paws, and if I hadn't already fallen in love with Ty, this would've sealed the deal.

"She's precious," I breathed. "So, you found her?"

"I saw her hiding under the shed the same night I last saw you. I started putting food out for her. I didn't know it was a girl until she finally came in, but she's decided she likes living where it's warm."

My heart ached a little at the sweetness. "Gee, Ty, I didn't take you as that much of a softie."

His cheeks flushed a little as he gave me a sheepish shrug. "I couldn't help it. I couldn't leave her out there. Winter is coming, and we've already had several frosts. I don't think she could survive on her own all winter."

He handed her over to me, and she immediately took interest in my hair, biting at it and purring as I stroked over the top of her head. Ty couldn't have known it, but this was the perfect distraction. Obviously, we would have that talk, but a sweet, playful kitten eased the tension clenching around my heart.

"Do you need anything to drink?" he asked as he rounded the kitchen counter to open the refrigerator.

"Just water."

In another moment, he was back at my side with two glasses of water in hand. "Let's sit." He gestured with his chin toward the couch.

That tension tightened around my heart again. I felt as if I were a spool of thread wound too tightly. I took a deep breath and followed him over, holding onto the little kitten. "So, her name's Silver?" I asked as we sat down.

He nodded. "I started calling her that before I knew she was a girl, and it stuck."

"Well, she *is* silver," I replied as I looked down at her and trailed my fingertips over her back.

She wiggled out of my arms, leaping off the sofa to pounce at an imaginary spot on the floor. I took a sip of the water Ty set on the coffee table in front of me, smiling when he slipped one of those red light pens out of his pocket. Silver was enchanted instantly. He didn't even have to pay attention. He idly shifted the pen in his hands while she chased the dot excitedly around the floor.

I reached for my water again, this time swallowing too much at once and sputtering. I got water all over my shirt and hands. He stood and quickly strolled to the kitchen, returning with a napkin and a paper towel.

"Sorry about that," I said after I cleaned up my little water mess.

"It's just water."

I could hear the echo of my heart beating in my ears and my palms were cold and clammy. If I'd thought it was hard to tell him I was pregnant, it was downright terrifying to tell him I wanted to have our baby. I didn't even know how he really felt.

But I was me, and I still had an impulsive streak. Diving right into an uncomfortable moment fit with that. Therapy had only honed that tendency. I swallowed. "So," I began, just as he did.

"Look—" His word crossed over mine.

Our words collided again. "Go ahead," I said, just as he offered, "Go ahead."

A nervous laugh bubbled up. "No, you go ahead," I insisted.

When we paused, each of us waiting, he cleared his throat. "I'm sorry. I didn't really know how to react when you told me. I hope you can understand I was a little shocked."

His gaze held mine steadily, and he looked so earnest that emotion rushed through me, and I thought I might cry. I wasn't much of a weepy girl, but the last few days, it sure felt like I was.

"I do understand. I was shocked too," I offered softly.

He cleared his throat again, resting his elbows on his knees and lacing his fingers together as he looked over at Silver. He still held the pen in one hand, idly rocking it between his fingers while she continued to pounce on the moving dot.

I waited, because I wasn't exactly sure how to say what I

needed to say next. He lifted his head, his smoky gaze meeting mine again and somehow managing to send my belly spinning in flips and heat chasing over my skin, even though he wasn't even trying, and I wasn't even thinking about sex.

I snorted.

"What?" he prompted.

"Nothing." He kept waiting, so I forged ahead, "I don't think I'll ever get used to the fact that when you look at me…" I took a nervous breath. "Let's just say it this way, the chemistry comes *real* easy with us."

A smile stretched slowly from one corner of his mouth to the other, sending sparks dancing through me. "That's one way to put it. I'd say it runs hot."

"Well, that too."

We stared at each other, and it almost felt as if something bloomed in the air between us. This time, it wasn't just chemistry. It wasn't something that hadn't been there before, it's just I'd never paused long enough to let the feeling take over.

His eyes sobered. "I'm not sure what you want, but I'm here for whatever it is," he said quietly.

I abruptly realized it was pretty important for me to tell him how I felt about him. I didn't know the order of what needed to be said first, but that felt pressing.

My heartbeat was galloping along so fast, I could hardly breathe. I abandoned the effort to convince myself I could get my nervous anxiety under control and stumbled ahead. "We haven't really talked about what this thing between us is," I began haltingly.

He had glanced down at Silver who was still pouncing on the little dot on the floor, and his head whipped back in my direction. There was a flare of warmth in his eyes that gave me a little courage.

"I love you." The words felt strange in my mouth, but my heart thumped out a resounding beat, and it was almost a relief to say it out loud. I was still freaking terrified.

His eyes widened slightly, but he didn't look away. After what felt like a moment that dragged on way too long, he unlaced his fingers, reaching over and catching my hand where it rested on my thigh. His big, warm palm curled around mine, and I looked down as his thumb started to stroke along the edge of my wrist.

"I didn't really know what to call us, but I'm glad I'm not alone," he said gruffly.

I dared a look at him. I found his lips curving in a slow smile again, and my belly swooped. My heartbeat felt like hands clapping inside. I still felt like I was waiting when he began with, "You always were that girl to me, you know?"

My throat was tight as I shook my head.

"I couldn't forget you," he explained. "I didn't feel like you broke my heart or anything. We were both pretty much on the same page back then. I was just looking for a good time."

He seemed to be waiting for me to say something, so I offered, "That's what I was looking for then too. It was a *really* good time with us."

There was a glint in his eyes. His thumb shifted its path, distracting me and disarming me when it brushed over the sensitive skin on the inside of my wrist.

"It still is a *really* good time with us," he offered, repeating my emphasis. "So, yeah, I never forgot you. Then, our worlds collided again, or something like that." He took a sharp breath in, almost as if he were steeling himself. "I never expected to fall for anyone, but I guess it was a foregone conclusion that I'd fall for you." My eyes were hot with tears as emotion crested inside me. "That was a really long way of saying I love you. Again," he added.

"You're not still upset with me about not telling you everything?" I didn't want to ask, but I had to.

He shook his head. "I was upset, but it was because I thought you didn't trust me. You're too important to let that stay between us. I hope—"

"I *do* trust you. I let my own embarrassment get in the way, and I'm sorry. You know everything now, so…" I shrugged sheepishly, and he nodded slowly.

The tears that had been threatening spilled over, jumping off my eyelashes onto my cheeks. Ty looked dismayed, releasing my hand and snagging the napkin that was still damp from the water I'd spilled. I grabbed it from him. "I seem to cry a lot the last few days. I suppose that's a side effect of a surprise pregnancy." I sniffled.

He didn't look comforted, his eyes searching mine. "I'm fine," I insisted.

Now, I was feeling foolish. Ty scooted closer on the couch, sliding his arm around my back, and I tucked my head against his shoulder. He had a great shoulder to burrow into when a person needed comfort. Specifically, me.

"Well, we got that big thing out of the way," he offered with a little chuckle as his fingers teased in the hair at my nape. The haphazard knot in my hair was falling loose, and he sent shivers down my spine when his fingers brushed along the sensitive skin of my neck.

"We did." I took a fortifying breath before peering up at him. "I want to have the baby. I know you probably don't—"

He shook his head sharply. "I didn't say that."

Nonplussed, I stared at him.

"Obviously, this is a surprise, as we've already established. I've had some time to think about it." He paused, and his swallow was audible as my heart pounded a staccato rhythm in my chest. "If we're in it together, I'd love to have a baby with you."

Another round of tears dove off my lashes as I blinked up at him. I still had the balled-up napkin in my hand and dabbed at my eyes quickly.

"Are you sure?" I asked.

Ty chuckled. "I'm only laughing because I'm nervous. Hell no, I'm not sure. There are not many things I'm sure about. Except I love you. Baby or not, I think you're the only person I could imagine trying to do this with. Also, it's really your call."

"It is?"

He nodded. "Maybe I *am* a man and a little slow on the uptake sometimes, but yes. It's your body, girl. You're the one who's got to make a human for nine months. And, you'll be the feeding station afterwards. It's also a lifetime commitment."

I burst out laughing, and Silver took that moment to skitter across the floor and leap wildly off my knees and back onto the floor.

"I guess that's one way to put it," I finally managed when I stopped laughing, wiping tears away once more.

"Just being honest." He shrugged.

I took a cleansing breath and let it out in a gust. "I guess I'd like it to be a decision we make together. If we're going to be together, that is."

"Oh, we're together," he said firmly. "If you want this baby, even though I'm pretty sure I have no fucking clue how to be a father and my parents' marriage is a horrible example of a relationship, I'm right there with you."

By luck or fate or whatever, this scary conversation turned out to be not so bad. Maybe it was because I scrambled up the nerve to tell Ty how I felt, but it helped a whole lot to know that he loved me too and that we were in this together.

"While my parents might have a better example of a marriage than yours, I don't know anything about being a mother." Surprising me, my next statement stumbled out. "You should know Bipolar Disorder can run in families."

Ty seemed way less stressed out about this than me and actually shrugged. "And?"

I threw my free hand up in the air. "Well, I feel like you should be informed."

He held my gaze quietly. "Consider me informed. I love you, and I can deal. I hear that things skated pretty out of control for you, but I love you exactly the way you are. My dad doesn't have Bipolar Disorder, and he can be a serious asshole. Everybody's got some shit to deal with, Belle."

"Maybe you should come with me to talk to my therapist about it before you decide."

Ty didn't even blink. "If you want me to go with you to see your therapist, sure, but that's not something I feel like I need to do. I love *you*." He lifted one of his big hands and palmed my cheek. "Did you miss that part?"

Then, I was crying—again—and we were kissing, only to be interrupted by Silver when she jumped on my lap and burrowed between us.

33

TY

TWO WEEKS LATER

"So, you're going for it?"

I looked over at Griff. I was standing in the storage room at Speakeasy, checking on our beer and liquor stock. We had a busy weekend coming up with the Colebury Beer Festival scheduled, and the weekend near Halloween had been busy so we were flying through stock. Although the events coordinator handled the catering, we always needed more alcohol because the events spilled over to the bar.

"Going for what?" I returned.

Griff leaned his big shoulder on the inside of the door. "Heard from Audrey that Belle is pregnant."

Oh, the joys of a small town. We missed that grace period of the first trimester until we told everyone. Belle told me she'd spilled the secret to Zara before she even told me. As it was, I didn't mind all that much. There was a peculiar sense of relief to owning up that Belle was the girl for me. Mind you, I was still fucking terrified about becoming a father.

My lips kicked up into a grin. "Yep. Kind of a surprise, but we're going for it."

Griff wasn't much on chatting. He held my gaze for a long moment and then gave a firm nod as he pushed away from the door. "Good move. If you know she's the one, lock her down quick."

I burst out laughing as he winked and continued down the hallway. I was still adjusting to this rather momentous shift in my life. The best part though? Belle spending every night at my place. I told her the other day she should chat with her landlady about subletting her lease. I was impatient for her to move in. Although I knew she loved me, this weird thing had happened where I wanted all of it at once.

"Where are we going?" Belle asked

I caught her hand as we walked out the back at Speakeasy. "To the river."

"We don't need to go to the river. That was our accidental encounter place," she offered with a saucy grin.

"Does that mean we can't go anymore?"

She shook her head quickly. "Of course not."

We fell quiet as we walked into the trees. Leaves crunched under our footsteps, covering the path in a thick carpet. Autumn was almost over. There was a hint of wood smoke drifting in the air from somewhere nearby, and Thanksgiving was coming up in a few weeks. Belle had asked me to go to her parents for Thanksgiving and even invited my sister and mother. She'd pointedly noted my father wasn't invited, although she'd graciously offered to have dinner with him somewhere if I wanted.

By the time we reached the bench, my heart was pounding hard enough to startle me. I felt as if I were back in college practicing my skating for games. Belle sat down, immediately swinging her feet.

"What is it?" she asked, a twitch of worry creasing her brow as she peered up at me.

Fuck, even my hands were sweaty. I hadn't played goalie in college for nothing. I could handle pressure, but this was a different kind of pressure.

I decided to barrel right through it. Reaching into my pocket, I fished out the small box. With a little advice from May, I'd gone to the local crystal shop and picked up a pretty carved wooden box for the ring. She thought it was a nice touch for Belle.

I sat down beside her and held out my hand as I flipped it open. Her eyes flew open wide and tears glittered on her cheeks in another second. She'd been more emotional since she'd been pregnant. That was definitely an interesting side effect.

"Oh, my God, what is this?" she whispered.

"Will you marry me?"

I'd actually tried to think of a different way to ask this but eventually discovered there was really no other way to ask such a simple question. At least, not for me. Belle stared at me, her luminous eyes still wide. A gust of wind blew through the trees, sending a lock of her hair over her cheek. Lifting a hand, I brushed it away and trailed my thumb along her jawline.

She took a shaky breath. "Are you sure?"

This didn't surprise me. I was learning Belle carried lots of doubts. She was so accustomed to always doing everything for herself that the idea someone might be there for her wasn't something she accepted easily.

"'Course I'm sure. I love you, and we're having a baby, so I didn't see any sense in waiting."

"What if something happens?" she asked, her voice thick with tears.

I knew what she was asking even though she didn't voice it specifically. We still hadn't made it through the first trimester, and she was worried.

"It doesn't change the fact that I love you and can't imagine spending the rest of my life with anyone but you. If you're not ready—" I began.

She shook her head quickly. "Yes. I'm ready. Yes!" She blinked again, her lashes damp with tears as she looked up at me. "I really didn't expect any of this."

As I slipped the ring on her finger, a simple platinum band, I murmured, "That makes two of us."

She laughed into our kiss, and I tugged her onto my lap. It was chilly, just enough that she shivered. Opening my coat, I rested my chin on her shoulder and wrapped her in it as we looked out over the water.

There were lots of things I didn't know, but loving Belle was easy.

BELLE

THE FOLLOWING AUTUMN

I lay in bed, staring at the beams above my head. For a moment, I was confused. I reached my arm over to where I thought I might find Ty sleeping beside me. But the sheets were almost cool with a hint of lingering warmth. That let me know he'd recently gotten up.

I rolled to my side, stretching before I kicked the covers off and got out of bed. After belting my robe around my waist, splashing cold water on my face and brushing my teeth in the bathroom, I walked into the main area of our place. Looking across the living room, my eyes landed on Ty. He held our baby, Theo, in one arm as he made coffee with his free hand. We'd named our son after my father.

"You're way too young for this," he was saying to Theo. "But it's absolutely necessary for me in the morning, so you're gonna have to deal. Plus, your mom expects it. She gave it up for nine months for you."

Tears stung my eyes, and my heart beat out a peculiar thump, a feeling associated solely with Ty and our son. Love was a funny thing. It felt soaring and freeing, but it carried risk with it because it meant so much and felt so fragile. There were still days I couldn't quite believe I had stumbled into this life.

Ty heard me as I crossed the room. He glanced over, and my pulse hummed in response. I still couldn't lay eyes on him without getting a little heated.

There were major benefits to falling in love with your hottest hookup. Nobody else even came close, and he still had the ability to drive me completely wild.

"Good morning, sunshine," he said when I stopped beside him.

Our baby squealed and greeted me with a smile of pure joy. I kissed Theo and then Ty as Ty tapped the start button on the coffee maker.

"I tried not to wake you up," he said as he curled an arm around my waist and pressed a kiss to my temple.

"I know, but I'm up anyway."

Theo wiggled in his arms. Ty moved away, crossing over to set him in his favorite rocker. Silver wound around my ankles when I propped my hips against the counter.

Ty crossed back over to me, resting his hands on either side of my hips. His eyes held mine, and my belly felt fluttery. Just as I opened my mouth to say something, he kissed me. In a hot second, my arms were winding around his neck and I could feel the press of his arousal against my hip.

I broke free, laughing breathlessly. "We have an audience."

His grin was sly as he straightened. "I think that's a permanent state of affairs, or at least for eighteen years."

I placed my palm on his chest, savoring the feel of his steady heartbeat. Ty was turning out to be an awesome father. He didn't mind getting up during the night, and if I got up to feed our baby, he sat with me. He also didn't mind changing diapers.

"I love you," I said suddenly.

"Ditto," he replied, something he said often. "What's your schedule today?"

"I need to come up with the specials for the week, so I'll be heading in by noon."

"Sweet. We can ride in together."

Even though we technically worked at the same place, we didn't see each other a whole lot, except in passing at the restaurant. It was too busy for both of us when we were there.

"I have an appointment with my doctor this morning," I added when he turned away as the coffee maker beeped.

"Oh, that's right. Did you want me to go with you?"

"You don't have to. I can handle it on my own," I replied.

Ty's eyes held mine. "I'll go. That way, I know the scoop."

I almost cried again. Babies and hormones and love seemed to have that effect. I really didn't expect him to shadow me at every appointment, but my heart swelled that he wanted to.

He filled a cup of coffee and handed it to me. I caught his hand, reeling him back to me for another kiss.

THE
END

ACKNOWLEDGMENTS

To Sarina: it's such an honor to write in this world - thank you for the opportunity! Gracious thanks to the team at Heart Eyes Press for their support and all-around awesomeness.

Thank you to my editor and proofreader for helping me make Heartwood the best story it could be. Many thanks to the early readers who catch any details I might miss.

To DBC for the journey & more, and to my dogs who are the best company when I'm plotting and writing.

xoxo
J.H. Croix